SHATTERED WHISPERS

LANTERN BEACH EXPOSURE
BOOK.2

CHRISTY BARRITT

CHAPTER
ONE

ABBY MENDEZ FUMBLED with her keys as she huddled outside the side entrance of the theater.

The chilling wind blasted against her, its strength nearly slamming her into the building. Earlier, she'd heard someone say gusts would hit nearly forty miles an hour today.

She believed it.

Finally, she found the key, jammed it into the lock, and twisted.

As a gale caught the door and flung it open, Abby practically stumbled inside the theater. Quickly, she fought Mother Nature as she struggled to shut the door behind her.

Finally, she managed to get it closed.

The theater was dark and silent, except for the muffled sounds of the storm outside.

She found the light switch and flipped it.

Dim fluorescents buzzed overhead as the historic schoolhouse-turned-theater came into sight. The scent of paint, ancient dust, and old wood filled her senses.

She loved this building, and being here always brought her a measure of comfort.

Theater was the place Abby had found acceptance and a stirring passion. She was so honored to have been entrusted with starting a troupe on this isolated barrier island off the North Carolina coast.

They were currently working on *The Legend of Lantern Beach*, a play Abby herself had written detailing the island's history—in the most entertaining way possible. The production, full of pirates and early settlers, would open for the summer season in six weeks, and she couldn't be happier about it.

Right now, Abby needed to work on the set. She had a few people helping her, but she worried everything wouldn't get done in time for opening night.

She strode past the seating area and onto the stage before pausing in front of one of the backdrops—an ocean scene. She frowned as she remembered her visit to the actual ocean earlier tonight.

Just an hour ago, Abby had finished a date with Raef Fallon. She could tell the tall, lanky, and slightly clueless man liked her.

But she didn't share his feelings. They had no chemistry, and . . . she wasn't particularly attracted to the pale blond with the quirky—and slightly off-putting—sense of humor.

Now, the two of them had to work together since he'd volunteered to run sound for her at the theater. He'd also offered to help her with the set tonight, but Abby had declined his assistance.

The two-and-a-half-hour date had been too much time spent with Raef as it was. Then, when he'd pushed for a second date, she'd been forced to tell him she wasn't interested in going out again.

She hated to do it—hated to hurt him. But she couldn't lead him on either because that would only leave him with more disappointment in the end.

Abby hoped things wouldn't become awkward between the two of them. But how could they not?

Immediately after the date, she'd created a new rule for herself: never date anyone involved with her productions. It seemed men were her poison, a trait that her mother had apparently passed on to her.

She'd thought the solution to her problems would be to date passive men. Yet she wasn't attracted to that type. Instead, she was drawn to men with strong personalities—the type who could often be controlling.

But no man would ever control her again. She

would be homeless and starving before she accepted the help of a supposedly well-intentioned man who simply wanted to dictate her future.

Never again.

She frowned, grabbed the supplies she'd tucked behind the stage earlier, and planted herself in front of the backdrop. A few minutes later, she began absently stroking her blue-paint-dipped brush on what would soon be the sky.

A sound echoed from inside the building, and she froze.

Was someone else here?

Her breath caught.

Only two other people had keys to this place—her assistant director, Danielle, and her stage manager, Devin. Abby knew for a fact neither of them were here. No other cars were in the parking lot, though she supposed someone could have walked here . . . Still, it seemed unlikely.

Her heart thumped harder.

She remained frozen on her knees, paintbrush in hand, as she listened for the sound again.

Several minutes later, silence still reigned.

It was probably the wind. The gusts were strong, and this old building was creaky.

Releasing her breath, she began painting the backdrop again.

But her nerves remained on edge.

They had been ever since Myrtle Beach . . . well, before that even. She thought by coming to Lantern Beach she could escape her trouble.

She couldn't.

Memories from her past haunted her every day.

The creak sounded again, loud enough this time that Abby flinched. The paintbrush flew from her hands.

She glanced down and saw streaks of blue on the glossy wood floor—the floor she'd just had redone less than a month ago. This was so typical for her life.

Abby grabbed an old rag she kept near the paint can and quickly cleaned the mess.

As she did, the gale smashed more debris into the building. Probably small branches, leaves, and sand. The wind on this barrier island was a force to be reckoned with.

Just then, a new sound cut through the air.

Was that a . . . a moan?

Abby's throat tightened until she could hardly breathe.

She swallowed hard before calling, "Hello?"

No answer.

Should she call the police?

No, that seemed like overkill. Especially since this could be nothing. It probably *was* nothing.

Rising, Abby gripped the paintbrush like a weapon as she crept toward the door leading behind the stage.

She hesitated as she stared at the exit, which had been painted black to blend with the walls.

She didn't want to open that door.

But she had no other choice.

This was her theater, after all. She could call for help, but she had an overactive imagination at times, especially considering what had happened here at Christmas.

Someone had vandalized the place and targeted her in an effort to shut the theater down. Thankfully, that person was no longer a threat. But the memories still haunted her.

Abby lifted a quick prayer before grabbing the door handle.

Slowly, she twisted.

Opened.

Stared.

Saw nothing.

Then she stepped into the dark hallway. She called this area the guts of the theater, the place where things moved and happened, but the audience never saw these inner workings.

She found the light switch and flicked it.

Illumination filled the narrow passageway.

The narrow, *empty* passageway—the sight of which seemed to confirm to her that she was over-reacting.

Gathering her courage, Abby continued down the corridor toward her office, which was tucked around the corner at the end.

So far, so good.

She had to force herself to put one foot in front of the other.

As she took another step, Abby realized she was holding the paintbrush out in front of her as if that might protect her. *Silly, girl. Assault with a deadly paintbrush isn't really a thing.*

Still, she didn't lower her arm.

She hadn't heard anything since she stepped back here.

Had the person who'd made that noise left the building?

Or were they hiding?

Abby didn't like the second option.

She still hoped this was all her overactive imagination. Or the wind. Or the old building creaking with age and aches.

Reaching her office door, she paused.

She thought for sure she'd left the room closed.

But the door was barely ajar.

Someone was *definitely* in this theater with her.

Holding the paintbrush up higher, she nudged the door with her foot. As the opening widened, a sliver of light from the hallway streaked across the floor of her office.

The beam illuminated something out of place.

She leaned closer.

It was a person.

Lying there.

In front of her desk.

She blinked as the man's face came into view.

Then a scream rose like scalding hot water vapor in her throat until a shrill sound escaped.

It was Raef.

Unmoving.

Eyes wide open.

Dead.

Just as Abby took a step back, a shadow appeared from the corner of the office.

The killer, she realized . . . he was still here.

And he stared at her as if she might be his next victim.

———

Hunter Bancroft pulled his jacket closer around him as the wind blasted into him like an invisible wrecking ball. The system moving through the area hadn't brought rain or storms, but the wind could knock a person over.

He wasn't going to let that stop him.

As per his normal routine, he was taking a long walk to blow off steam and reflect on all the changes of the past few years. Walking was his therapy.

Lantern Beach seemed like a good temporary stop on his journey. He didn't know how long he'd be here working for Blackout, a private security agency. But he'd at least stay until he figured out his next move.

Because life had thrown him several curveballs that he still hadn't recovered from.

As Hunter paced the gravel road, he spotted the old theater in the distance.

He'd gone to see the Christmas play there back in December. Several of his friends had been part of the production. Despite his grumpiness about attending, Hunter had found himself enjoying the play entirely more than he'd anticipated.

The leader of the theater troupe, Abby Mendez, had amused him with her dramatic antics and fake accents—all done with a good dose of humor and a wide smile.

The woman was definitely his polar opposite. He was all shadow. She was all limelight.

He didn't like drama. He rarely smiled. And he *hated* being the center of attention.

Abby's image filled his head. Slender figure. Olive skin. Dark hair. Big brown eyes.

He would guess her to be Italian—not only because of her looks but because she talked fast with lots of hand movements.

Her laugh was infectious, even if Hunter had promised himself to remain immune to the sound.

Laughing was a distraction.

That's what he told himself, at least. Ever since Stephanie's death, his outlook had been bleaker than it should.

He was working on it, however. He'd been well into the healing process when he'd discovered Stephanie had wiped out their entire savings account a week before she died.

Why? Was she going to leave him? Was someone blackmailing her?

He didn't know, and he hadn't been able to find any answers.

Not yet.

But he was still working on it.

As Mother Nature paused long enough to suck in a breath before releasing another gust of wind, a new sound cut through the darkness.

A scream.

Hunter's back muscles tightened.

The noise had come from the theater.

He only saw one car parked out front, so he didn't think practice was going on or that the sound was part of rehearsal for an upcoming play.

No, someone was in trouble.

He sprinted toward the building and reached the front.

The doors there were locked.

Instead, he darted to the side of the building and tried another door.

His lungs loosened—but only for a moment—when he discovered this door was unlocked.

He rushed inside and paused in the auditorium, quickly noting the scent of fresh paint in the air.

As the door slammed shut behind him—carried by the wind, he scanned the place.

He didn't see anyone, only empty seats and a half completed set on the stage.

He listened for any telltale sounds of what had happened here.

Nothing.

Then the sound of another door slamming filled the air.

The sound had come from backstage.

Hunter darted up the stairs onto the stage, rushed toward the back, and jerked open the door.

As he glanced at the end of the hallway, he spotted Abby standing in the corner. She held onto the wall as if she might topple over. Her eyes were wide, and her skin was deathly pale. She gripped a paintbrush in her hand, part of the baby blue from the bristles splattered on her white T-shirt.

"Abby?"

She pointed behind him. "A man. He was here. You must have just missed him."

Hunter glanced over his shoulder as he contemplated his options.

Then he looked at Abby again. "Are you okay?"

She opened her mouth to speak but closed it again.

The woman appeared to be speechless.

That was never a good sign.

"Abby?" Hunter repeated.

"He's . . . dead," she finally murmured.

Concern pulsed through him. "Who's dead?"

"Raef. In my office."

Suddenly, Hunter forgot about chasing after the man who'd just escaped. He pulled out his phone and dialed Police Chief Cassidy Chambers. He explained the situation, and she promised to be right out. She and her guys had a better chance of catching the person who'd done this. They could spread out and strategically search the area.

For now, Hunter needed to make sure that this Raef guy was actually dead and not simply in need of medical help.

He hurried toward Abby. "Where?"

She led him to her office and stood stiffly near the doorway, almost as if she couldn't make herself step inside the room.

Hunter gently nudged her aside and flipped on the light.

His breath caught when he saw the body sprawled on the floor.

He put his finger to the man's throat.

No pulse.

The man was definitely dead.

Bruises had already formed around his neck.

A chill washed through Hunter at the sight.

He'd seen this guy around town a couple of times—including earlier tonight—but Hunter didn't really know him. Still, death meant grief . . . for someone.

And a death like this? It also meant danger.

He rose and turned toward Abby, concerned about her well-being. "Are you sure you're okay?"

She still gripped the paintbrush, holding it as if it were a weapon.

Hunter gently eased it from her hand and placed it on the edge of her desk.

He held her cold hands as he stared her in the

eye. "It's going to be okay, Abby. Let's get you away from here. We need to preserve the crime scene."

She nodded but the motion looked stiff, and her eyes looked glazed.

As Hunter led her away, he glanced at the end of the hallway and saw an emergency exit near the backstage door.

That must be where the killer had escaped.

Tension rippled through Hunter's back muscles.

He didn't know what was going on.

But he didn't like the fact there was a murderer loose on this island.

ABBY KNEW she should be grateful that Hunter had arrived when he did. She knew that he'd been a real godsend in the midst of her turmoil.

But he was also the type of guy she tried to stay away from—he was the exact kind of person who was bad for her. He was overly strong, type A, brooding, and . . . controlling.

When she'd first met that man, she'd been taken with him. Thankfully, she'd quickly come to her senses.

She set those thoughts aside right now. They weren't important.

Raef's death was.

Police Chief Chambers—Cassidy to Abby, who knew her because of mutual friends—and Officer

Dillinger had shown up probably five minutes after Hunter's call.

They'd instructed her to sit in the auditorium's front-row seats. She hadn't argued. Her legs felt as if they might give out on her.

Cassidy sat beside her while Officer Dillinger documented the crime scene.

Hunter kept pace with the officer, pointing out the path the killer had most likely taken.

It was probably better Hunter wasn't here beside Abby. He tended to make her feel self-conscious. Not that he meant to do so.

Abby's feelings were mostly because she'd had such a huge crush on him when they first met. She'd tried flirting with him, but her actions hadn't been reciprocated. Once she'd realized he wasn't interested, she'd simply avoided him.

However, she did run into Hunter one day when she'd been walking on the beach. He'd taken the opportunity to tell her what she should and shouldn't be doing. That was when she'd realized he was just like every other guy she'd dated—and regretted.

If Abby was smart, she'd stay away from any relationships . . . or potential relationships, anyway. Her last two had been abysmal.

More than abysmal.

They'd been a stark awakening to reality—real-life fairy tales didn't exist.

Cassidy turned toward her, notepad in hand, as her intelligent eyes soaked in every detail. "Can you tell me what happened?"

The woman's blonde hair was pulled into a bun at the back of her head, and she wore a blue shirt, jeans, and a blazer. Abby had quickly come to admire the woman. She was dedicated to God, her family, and this island—and she balanced it all effortlessly. So it seemed, at least.

Abby ran through tonight's events.

Cassidy frowned as Abby finished. "Do you have any idea what Raef was doing here?"

"I have no idea. I mean, I didn't even see his car out front, so I didn't think anyone was here." She paused. "Although . . . I did mention I was coming here this evening to work on the set. I told Raef I didn't need his help. I suppose he might have come because he knew I'd be here . . ."

"That's possible."

Her thoughts continued to race. "However, even if Raef *was* here for some reason, he shouldn't be in my office. I usually keep it locked."

"When was the last time you saw Raef before you found him tonight?"

"About an hour ago." Abby's cheeks heated. "For

the past few weeks, he'd repeatedly asked me if I wanted to go on a date. I kept saying no. But finally, I caved and said yes." Abby pushed a lock of hair behind her ear as she gathered herself. "The two of us went to dinner earlier this evening."

"What changed your mind?"

She shrugged, now regretting her choices. "I decided to be more open-minded. In theory, at least. But it was clear to me within the first few minutes it was a mistake to go out with him."

"Why do you say that?"

"There was no spark. No . . . anything. I just didn't feel like we had any chemistry. The heart knows what the heart knows, right?"

"I understand. Did Raef say anything strange? That he was having problems with anyone?"

Abby shook her head. "Our conversation was pretty generic and slightly awkward. But he didn't tell me about any peculiar conflicts—nothing serious, at least."

Cassidy shifted. "What about the man in the shadows? Can you tell me anything about him?"

Abby shivered as memories flooded her. Memories of seeing him step out of the darkness. Memories of the menacing look in his eyes.

Memories of his silence.

"I didn't get a good look at him. He was wearing a ski mask."

"Did he say anything?" Cassidy asked.

"No, he just stared at me. It was weird. It was almost like he wanted to say something but didn't— or couldn't. I'm not sure. But the silence was almost more unnerving than if he'd just talked."

"Was he holding any type of a weapon?"

"Not that I saw."

Cassidy nodded. "Okay, what else can you tell me?"

"Nobody was supposed to be here tonight. Maybe this guy thought he'd have the place to himself, to do whatever he intended to do." Her voice cracked. "He must've killed Raef, and then hid when he heard me come backstage. When he realized I'd seen Raef's body, he stepped out of the darkness."

She shivered again as the memories hit her. Had those noises she'd heard been Raef's demise?

Cassidy's eyes narrowed. "Then what?"

"Then I heard the door at the side of the theater open. It was Hunter. The killer must have heard him too. He shoved me to the floor and ran."

"Sounds like he was rough with you. Are you sure you don't want to be checked out by a paramedic?" Cassidy scanned Abby again.

"I'm fine. Just shaken up."

Cassidy narrowed her eyes with thought as she glanced at her notepad. "One more question. What can you tell me about Raef? Where was he from? Has he ever been married? Where did he work?"

Abby sucked in a deep breath as she tried to gather her thoughts.

"I don't know a lot about him, but I do know he turned thirty last month. He came here from Wisconsin. He just started working a maintenance job for . . . what's the name of that place?" She snapped her fingers. "Oh, I know. Ocean Essence."

Cassidy's eyes widened at the mention of the lab.

Abby realized that the reference to Ocean Essence had caught the police chief's attention.

Was there something going on with the cosmetics research laboratory that had recently opened new facilities on Lantern Beach? Abby had met a few scientists around town who worked there. They all seemed friendly enough.

One of them, a woman named Rachel Atwood, had even become a regular at Beach Bound Books and Beans. Abby and the girls had mentioned possibly adding her to their book club.

Abby couldn't imagine why or how the lab might be connected with anything that had happened here tonight.

But she just wanted all of this to be over.

She wanted the show to go on. For Raef to still be alive. And for trouble to stop following her.

———

Hunter inspected the theater with Officer Dillinger, searching for any clues the killer may have left behind. Doc Clemson, the town doctor and coroner, was here examining the body before taking it to the morgue.

It wasn't that Hunter was an expert at looking at crime scenes, but he *had* been a Navy SEAL for twelve years. He had an eye for trouble and for detail.

The one thing he knew for sure was that he didn't like the scene in front of him.

As he searched backstage, an image of earlier tonight filled his mind.

He'd been walking on the boardwalk, leaving the bake shop one of his friends owned, when he'd seen Abby and Raef eating together at a seafood restaurant.

Abby had been laughing at something Raef said, and Raef was positively glowing as he'd sat at the table across from her.

Something about seeing the two of them together bothered him.

Which was stupid.

Abby was all sunshine, and Hunter was a self-proclaimed grump.

So his reaction made absolutely no sense.

Abby was free to date whomever she wanted. The two of them weren't even friends. And he wasn't interested in dating again.

Either way, Hunter was worried about her.

This whole situation left him feeling uneasy.

He'd overheard Abby telling Cassidy about when the killer had stepped out of the shadows.

Even more bothersome was the fact that the killer might now see Abby as a threat.

Hunter kept that thought in the back of his mind, not wanting to voice it out loud yet and scare Abby.

But there was a good chance she was still in danger.

Cassidy rose, appearing to be finished questioning Abby. "I don't feel like you should be driving yourself home tonight after all this. How about you let us give you a ride? We should be finishing up in another thirty minutes or so."

Hunter stepped out from backstage. "I can drive her home now."

Abby glanced up at him in surprise. "I don't want you to go out of your way."

"It's no problem. If I were you, I wouldn't want to

hang around this place any longer than necessary—not until the scene is cleaned up, at least."

Abby glanced at Cassidy for her approval.

The police chief nodded. "That's fine with me. It's your choice."

Finally, after a moment of contemplation, Abby nodded. "Okay then. It would be nice to get out of here."

A surprising relief filled him. "If it's okay with you, I'll need to drive your car. I was taking a walk when I heard you scream, so I don't have my vehicle with me."

"Of course. But you need the magic touch to get it started." Abby shrugged as if embarrassed by her car.

Hunter had seen her sedan before. The clunker was at least twenty years old with lots of dents and bumps on its faded red paint.

But he didn't care what kind of car she drove, as long as it got her where she needed to go.

After talking to Cassidy a few more minutes, he and Abby stepped outside into the dark and windy night. Hunter checked his watch. It was already 9:30.

He glanced around, making sure danger didn't linger nearby.

He didn't see anything, but the darkness could conceal a lot. He needed to remain on guard.

Abby handed him her keys, and Hunter tucked her inside before climbing behind the wheel.

He tried to crank the engine. It took three tries before it turned over.

Finally, he pulled away from the theater. "You'll have to give me directions to your house."

"Unfortunately, that's the last place I want to be tonight. The thought of staying there alone . . ." Abby trembled again. "If you wouldn't mind, I'd like to stop by Tali's place. Maybe she wouldn't mind if I slept over there."

That sounded like a good idea to him. "Your wish is my command."

CHAPTER
THREE

ABBY'S MIND raced as she and Hunter headed down the quiet island road.

Darkness surrounded them, and she couldn't stop looking for movement in the shadows in the reeds and behind trees and near the homes they passed. At any minute, it seemed as if that man might reappear to finish what he'd started. That he might hunt her down.

That he might finally speak—and she'd finally hear his cruel voice and threats.

Had he kept silent because she might recognize his voice?

The thought unsettled her even more.

It didn't matter how hard she willed herself to stop trembling, the shakes wouldn't cease. Fear seemed to fill her, right alongside the blood in her veins and the air in her lungs.

Every time she closed her eyes, she relived everything that had happened tonight.

She would be replaying that scene for a very long time.

"I've seen my fair share of dead bodies as a Navy SEAL." Hunter's voice pulled her from her thoughts. "It's tough. You don't have to pretend like it's not, especially not for my sake."

Abby rubbed her arms, grateful he was trying to be cordial. "Thank you."

"I'm sorry you lost Raef tonight."

She did a double take at Hunter, unsure if she'd heard him correctly. "What do you mean, I lost him?"

"I know he meant a lot to you." Hunter shrugged—but not before casting her a glance that made it clear he was concerned about her current mental state.

"Raef was a nice guy, but I don't know if I'd say he meant a lot to me. I mean, not to sound insensitive toward a man who was just murdered, but . . ."

Hunter glanced at her again, a new emotion washing through his gaze. "I see."

That was weird.

Why would Hunter even think that Raef meant a lot to her?

It was like she'd said—she liked the guy as a person. He was a decent human and had some talents as the sound tech for the show.

But as far as romance? There was absolutely, positively, no-doubt-about-it nothing between them.

Why would Hunter think there was?

Several minutes later, they pulled into a lot across from Beach Bound Books and Beans, the bookstore/coffee shop her friend Tali MacArthur owned. Abby had tried to call, but Tali hadn't answered.

Even so, Tali had proven many times that if Abby ever needed anything Tali would be there for her. Abby felt comfortable dropping in.

Hunter climbed out and put his hand on the small of Abby's back as he nodded toward the store across the street.

But Abby noticed how he glanced around as they crossed the street.

He still thought this killer could be lingering close, didn't he?

That thought sent another chill through her.

Why couldn't trouble leave her alone . . . at least, for a little while?

———

Hunter would never admit it, but part of him was relieved to learn that Raef wasn't special to Abby.

He wasn't sure why he felt that way. The reaction didn't make sense.

He hadn't dated since Stephanie died three years ago, and he had no desire to. Instead, he'd been content concentrating solely on his job.

He'd been committed to his marriage, but he had to admit that he and Stephanie had more than their fair share of struggles. His schedule combined with her proclivity for partying had been a harsh combination. Looking back, they'd rushed into marriage too quickly. They'd made too many mistakes.

Mostly, however, Hunter knew that he'd failed her. He'd wanted to make things better.

Before they'd had a chance to figure things out, she was gone.

And she'd died with secrets—secrets Hunter was still trying to uncover.

His gaze drifted back to Abby.

When he first arrived on the island, Abby had flirted with him every chance she got. She'd been cute. Adorable, really. But he wasn't interested in her.

In *anyone*, for that matter.

That statement still stood.

The best way to protect his heart was by remaining single. He believed in planning and goals

—and staying away from any romantic entanglements seemed like the best course of action.

He escorted Abby across the street. Since it was afterhours, the store was closed, and she rang the bell at the front door.

As they waited, Hunter glanced around again, still on the lookout for trouble.

He didn't see anything suspicious.

Instead, he reflected on the last part of the conversation he'd overheard between Cassidy and Abby at the theater. Abby had mentioned that Raef had just started working for Ocean Essence in their maintenance department.

There had been a lot of chatter around the island about the cosmetics company. Blackout had recently been contracted to do some security work there, guarding the outside of the property around the clock.

He wasn't sure how he felt about the place. Many thought the presence of the lab on such a secluded island was suspicious.

He didn't know enough about them to draw any conclusions yet.

But he did store that fact about Raef in the back of his mind.

Finally, the door opened, and Tali stood there holding Sugar, her Westie, in her arms.

In her mid-sixties, the woman maintained a youthful appearance, almost reminding Hunter of Goldie Hawn with her blonde hair and lithe figure. He'd enjoyed chatting with her the few times he'd been browsing titles in the bookstore.

The woman's eyes lit with alarm when she saw Abby.

Mac, her husband, appeared behind her. He was the Lantern Beach mayor and former police chief—a staple in the area and a legend in his own right.

"What's going on?" Mac's voice sounded tense. "Is everything okay?"

"I'm hoping I can stay here tonight." Abby's voice quivered as she spoke.

Tali glanced from Abby to Hunter as questions filled her gaze. "Of course, you can. What's going on?"

"It's Raef . . . he's been murdered!" With those words, Abby fell into Tali's motherly embrace.

THIRTY MINUTES LATER, even though it was nearing eleven at night, the book club gathered in the cozy seating area of the shop downstairs.

These ladies had become like family to Abby, and she was grateful for each of them. When she'd called for this emergency meeting, no one had hesitated to come.

Tali was the matriarch of the group with her wisdom and nurturing spirit. Abby's own mother had passed when Abby was only twenty-one, and Tali somehow felt like an endearing fill-in.

Then there was Serena Lavinia, who was both a reporter and the island's ice cream lady. She was strange and quirky at times but a loyal friend. Despite her sometimes ditzy antics, she really was smart—as well as very persistent and headstrong.

Finally, there was Cadence Garth, who'd come to the island to help out her cousin, Lisa Dillinger, who ran the popular restaurant The Crazy Chefette. Cadence helped with both taking care of Lisa's two kids and waitressing at the restaurant. Cadence was quiet, loved reading, and seemed almost mysterious at times.

When Abby needed a friend who gave solid advice, Cadence was her girl.

Tali's niece, Maisie, had joined them recently, but she was out of town on a trip this week. Tali had insisted that Abby could stay in Maisie's room while she was gone.

With warm drinks in their hands, the questions began pouring from her friends like hot coffee from a carafe on a cold day.

Abby curled her legs under her and recounted tonight's events. Sugar seemed to sense her distress, and he'd jumped into her lap. She stroked the dog's head as she spoke.

More questions followed, questions she tried to answer.

But there was so little she knew at this point.

Mostly, she knew Raef was dead. That he'd been strangled in her office. That the killer had been hiding and probably would have murdered Abby also if Hunter hadn't arrived when he did.

Abby's trembles started again, stronger now. They were so bad that tea spilled from the edges of her cup, and she had to place her drink on the table beside her.

After a brief lull in the conversation, Serena shifted and said, "Hunter, huh?"

A sparkle twinkled in her eyes as she said his name.

Abby had never talked about Hunter to her friends, but they were astute enough to notice she'd had a crush on the man. *Had*—past tense. No more. Men and romance were always a mistake.

"He hates me." Abby crossed her arms over her chest.

She hadn't exactly meant to say those words out loud. But they were true.

Whenever the guy looked at her, he scowled. Abby tried to make him laugh, and he only stared at her as if she'd lost her mind. She'd tried to engage in conversation, and he'd shrugged her off.

She'd even flirted and had gotten nowhere.

She was halfway shocked he had helped her tonight.

She mentally shook her head. No, that wasn't correct.

She wasn't shocked about that.

Just because he didn't laugh at her jokes or

engage in conversation didn't mean he wasn't a good guy. He was a former Navy SEAL, for goodness' sake. He'd put his life on the line for this country.

That alone made him a good guy.

Plus, he was friends with Cassidy's husband, Ty. And Ty wouldn't have anyone as his friend who was less than honorable.

Abby hated having such mixed feelings about the man, but she couldn't figure him out. And figuring out people was what she did best.

"How could anyone hate you?" Tali gave her a motherly glance.

"He looks at me like I'm off my rocker." Abby did a half eye roll. "Besides, the two of us are total opposites."

That was just as well. After Nelson and Michael, Abby should run far, far away from any romantic entanglements.

Her relationships with both of the men had been disasters.

They were the reasons she'd come here to Lantern Beach.

To get away from the drama.

As an actress, Abby loved drama—but only on the stage and not in real life.

When she glanced at the window, a movement outside caught her eye.

A man's shadow.

Her breath caught.

What if the killer had followed her here?

What if he wanted to finish what he'd started?

As if to confirm her fears, Sugar's hair stood on end, and the dog began to growl.

Before Abby could stop it, a scream escaped her lips.

———

Hunter hadn't left the boardwalk after taking Abby to the bookstore.

He'd decided to linger a while longer. He knew Tali would have invited him to stay inside, but he didn't want to impose.

Instead, he'd called for a ride. His colleague Axel Hendrix said he needed to wrap up his shift at Ocean Essence, but he'd be there before midnight. Hunter had told him that was fine.

Hunter had wanted to keep an eye on things for a while anyway. Wanted to make sure trouble hadn't followed Abby to Tali's place.

As he waited, he'd remained in the shadows.

Maybe he was being paranoid. But a bad feeling lingered in his gut.

The feeling that Abby could still be in trouble.

He didn't want to scare her by lurking near the shop. That's why he remained out of sight.

Hunter crossed his arms as he watched the store.

He spotted Abby cozied up inside with her book club ladies.

The four of them were quite the force around town and seemed like four peas in a pod, as the saying went, despite their varying personalities and ages. He watched them all now as they hugged each other and sipped their tea.

A moment of longing ached inside him.

He had a good brotherhood with his colleagues at Blackout. But social situations demanded a different kind of camaraderie.

Stephanie had been the social one who'd set up dinner dates with friends and small get-togethers at the house.

Hunter hadn't realized how much he'd miss those times until they were gone.

Though other friends had tried to keep in touch with him after Stephanie's death, nothing had been the same. Eventually, their calls had dropped off.

Hunter didn't blame them. He hadn't been very good at keeping up either.

Besides, Stephanie's friends hadn't always been the best influence. One of them knew what her secret was. Knew what she'd been up to.

He'd put in calls to several of them to no avail. No one admitted to knowing anything about the missing money from their savings account.

The only other person he could think of who might know was Jenny, Stephanie's best friend. But Jenny wasn't returning his calls.

Hunter wasn't going to give up. He would figure out what had happened to that money.

He feared Stephanie had been in trouble . . . and that she hadn't turned to him.

A sense of failure pressed into him.

He stiffened when he saw movement across the street.

Was that . . . someone lurking on the side of the store?

Just as the thought crossed his mind, a scream sounded from inside the bookstore.

He'd recognize that voice anywhere.

Abby.

"Hey!" Hunter yelled as he darted across the street.

The man sprinted down the alley, headed toward the ocean.

Hunter followed behind him, careful to stay on guard.

As Hunter reached the corner of the building, he paused.

He looked around but didn't see anyone.

Which way had the guy gone?

Before he could take another step, something pricked his neck.

Electricity charged through him.

Stunned, Hunter fell to the ground.

The guy had a Taser, he realized.

The device had rendered Hunter immobile.

As the black-clad figure disappeared into the distance, anger surged through Hunter.

He'd catch this guy, he vowed.

If it was the last thing that he did.

CHAPTER
FIVE

"WHAT'S GOING ON DOWN HERE?" Mac thundered down the stairs of the bookstore from the apartment above.

Abby gripped Cadence's arm—she'd been the closest person to grab—as fear pulsed through her. "I saw someone right outside the window. Then I heard a yell. I'm not sure what's going on."

Yet she thought she did know.

The killer was here.

He'd found her.

He'd come back to finish what he started.

Mac pulled his gun from his holster—he always had one on him, it seemed. Probably a habit from back in his days as chief of police. "Everyone, stay here."

Then, with muscles bristled, he stepped outside.

Abby saw the concern on Tali's face as he left. She was worried about Mac—and rightfully so.

Whoever was outside could be dangerous.

The minutes seemed to stretch by in silence as they all waited for an update.

Abby wanted to run to the window. To peer out. To get a glimpse of what could be happening.

Yet she couldn't move from her seat. Fear froze her in place.

Finally, several minutes later, Mac appeared in the doorway.

But he wasn't alone.

His arm was around someone, almost as if holding up an injured comrade after battle.

Abby's heart lodged in her throat as the man's face came into view.

"Hunter?" She sprang to her feet.

He looked dazed and almost out of it as he glanced at her.

Then she saw the scrapes on his hands.

What had happened?

Mac helped Hunter to a chair, and Hunter lowered himself there.

The ladies stared at him before shifting their gazes to stare at Mac instead.

"Mac?" Tali rubbed her throat as she waited for an explanation.

"Hunter saw someone lurking outside the shop and chased him. When he went around the corner, the guy tased him."

Abby gasped at the update. "What?"

Hunter nodded, still looking out of sorts. No doubt the effects of the Taser were still wearing off. She'd read about them in a book once, and she had no desire to ever experience that kind of jolt to her system.

"I tried to catch him and put an end to this." Hunter rubbed his head where he must have fallen. "But the guy was obviously anticipating trouble. In fact, I'll need to tell Cassidy to check for Taser marks on Raef's body as well. It could have been how this guy subdued Raef before he . . ." He didn't finish his statement.

Abby's heart pumped harder. She could fill in the blanks.

"What were you doing outside?" Abby studied his face, truly curious about why he'd stayed nearby. She'd told him goodbye nearly an hour and a half ago. It was almost midnight now, and the wind was still biting out there.

"I'm waiting for my ride. I decided to keep an eye on things as I did."

"You should've come inside." A wrinkle of concern formed on Tali's brow.

Hunter shrugged. "I figured you girls needed your time together, and I didn't want to interrupt that. I don't mind the cold—or waiting."

A surge of gratitude filled Abby.

Hunter had gone out of his way tonight because of her.

She'd be forever grateful for that.

But an even greater realization remained.

The person who'd killed Raef had been watching her this evening. Maybe waiting to strike.

Why else would he have been outside the book shop?

That had to be him, right?

Abby shivered again.

How would she ever resume her normal life?

———

Hunter hadn't liked admitting to Abby and Mac that this guy had caught him by surprise.

He was usually at the top of his game. Not many people got a jump on him.

But he hadn't anticipated that Taser.

Now the guy had gotten away . . . again.

His jaw hardened at the memory.

He needed to decompress out of everyone's

watchful eye, and he was grateful when Axel arrived to pick him up five minutes later.

He told everyone good night, glad that Mac would be nearby to keep an eye on Abby.

Then he climbed into the SUV Axel had borrowed from Blackout—Hunter had no desire to go double on Axel's motorcycle—and they took off back to the Blackout headquarters on the other end of the island.

Axel was another former SEAL. The man was tall with lean muscles, a devil-may-care attitude, and a rebellious gaze. His dark hair always looked messy— just the way Axel liked it.

Despite their differences, the man had become a good friend to Hunter since Hunter started working for Blackout five months ago.

As they headed toward headquarters, Hunter filled Axel in on tonight's events.

"Well, your day has been a lot more interesting than mine." Axel played the drums with his thumbs on the steering wheel. "All I did was stand guard outside Ocean Essence."

Ocean Essence had caused quite a stir on the island about a month ago when one of the employees there had been arrested for murder. The death hadn't occurred on the island, but plenty of suspicious activity had ensued.

The company was working hard to restore its

reputation with the locals and had even sponsored a family fun day on the boardwalk, complete with free hot dogs, hamburgers, and other treats as well as pony rides and a small concert.

Hunter's pulse spiked at the mention of the company. "Is that usually a busy place at night?"

"Sometimes. Tonight was mundane. Not my favorite job. I really feel like they could hire a Rent-A-Cop to get what they need. But they want Blackout."

"In other words, they only want the best for their company."

Axel shrugged. "I suppose."

"Have you heard of anything interesting that might be happening there?"

Axel raised his eyebrows. "Why would you ask that?"

Axel's voice made it clear he was egging Hunter on, trying to force him to voice his suspicions aloud.

"I try not to believe rumors, but the place has quite the reputation," Hunter finally said.

Some of the glib left Axel's voice as he shrugged again. "I wish I had something specific to tell you, but I don't. Lots of people coming and going. A suspicious car drove past a couple of times. That's about it."

"A suspicious car?" Now that was interesting.

"I called it in, but the vehicle was gone by the time the police got there."

"What made it suspicious?"

Axel let out a breath. "Just the way the guy was driving. The windows were tinted. He was going slow as if he was looking for someone. When he saw me, he quickly drove away."

Hunter chewed on that a moment. "It could just be someone who's curious after everything that happened."

Axel shrugged again. "Could be. But it's our job to remain cautious. You haven't had a shift over there yet?"

"Not yet." But Hunter might be requesting one soon. "Did you ever see a man named Raef Fallon there? He worked maintenance."

"I can't say I did." Axel did a double take at him. "He's the guy who died, right? Wait . . . you think Ocean Essence has something to do with his death?"

"I have no idea," Hunter said. "But Raef worked there, and someone murdered the guy in cold blood. If I hadn't gotten there when I did . . ."

"Then they might have gotten Abby also," Axel finished.

Hunter's jaw tightened when he heard the words voiced aloud. "Exactly."

"I'll keep my eyes and ears open for you, just in case."

"Thanks," Hunter muttered.

Something was going on, and he didn't like the feeling lingering in his gut.

Trouble had arrived on the island, and Hunter was going to do everything in his power to prevent anyone else from getting hurt.

CHAPTER
SIX

POLICE CHIEF CASSIDY CHAMBERS hadn't made it to the station yet this morning.

Instead, she'd swung by Beach Bound Books and Beans. She wanted to check on Abby, but the woman was still sleeping when she arrived.

Mac had let her inside and locked the door behind them. Tali was already prepping the coffee bar for the day, and she fixed them some warm drinks.

Cassidy and Mac found a little table in the corner to chat. Normally, Cassidy would be careful where she had these types of conversations.

But she knew this place was private. It didn't open for business for another twenty minutes.

"How's Abby?" Cassidy stared at Mac across the table.

He'd called her last night to let her know what had happened with Hunter. Cassidy had sent two of her officers out to look for anyone suspicious, but the guy who'd tasered Hunter was long gone.

"She's still shaken, as you can imagine. I worry about her."

"Me too. I don't know why the killer would have come back."

"Unless maybe Raef wasn't the target."

Cassidy frowned. She'd thought of that also. "That's definitely a possibility."

Mac shifted. "Any leads on the murder?"

"Official cause of death was strangulation."

Mac's eyebrows shot up. "That's unusual in this day and time. Any evidence left behind?"

"There were some footprints we found outside— we're keeping them on file, just in case. We're continuing to look at security footage from local homes and businesses, but so far there's been nothing."

He clicked his tongue in thought. "That's too bad."

"We did, however, find Taser marks on his chest."

"Taser marks? Just like with Hunter."

"Exactly. The guy who attacked him last night is most likely the same person who killed Raef."

"That's very interesting. You'll catch a break sometime."

"We will. We just have to be patient—which isn't easy when there's a killer on the loose." Cassidy frowned before shifting. "However, Raef *did* work at Ocean Essence, which I find very interesting."

Mac raised his eyebrows, curiosity filling his gaze. "Is that right? Please, share more."

"Turns out Raef worked maintenance for the company. When I talked to Raef's roommate, he shared that Raef had some type of confrontation with one of the employees there only a couple of days ago."

"Interesting . . ."

"Isn't it?"

"I'm going to head over to talk with them later," Cassidy finished. "I want to hear about Raef's terms of employment and talk to this guy he had the argument with."

"Good idea. I have another interesting update for you," Mac said before taking a sip of his coffee, almost as if he wanted the dramatic pause to build her anticipation.

"What's that?"

He lowered his voice. "The book club ladies either have already or are planning on hiring Hunter to protect Abby."

"What?" Cassidy let out a strangled chuckle. "Ty didn't say anything about that."

Mac glanced at his watch. "If I had to guess, Serena is probably calling Ty and Colton right now to see if they can get him to do the job."

Cassidy shifted as she let that revelation sink in. "So you're telling me that Serena and the rest of the ladies are going to hire Hunter specifically to act as a bodyguard for Abby?"

"We're worried about her," Tali piped in before shrugging apologetically. "I'm sorry. I'm not trying to listen in on the conversation, but I couldn't help but hear."

Cassidy nodded slightly, not surprised that Tali heard them. "*That's* going be interesting. The two seem like total opposites—the perfect pairing to drive each other crazy."

Hunter was a tough nut to crack. He always wore the same guarded expression and offered very little information about his past.

Ty had told her once that Hunter had lost his wife three years ago in a car accident. Hunter had been blanketed with grief for a long time following that. Maybe even still.

Cassidy also thought it was interesting that the ladies had specifically asked for Hunter. Why was that?

She had a feeling she knew.

Were these ladies trying to do some matchmaking in the middle of bodyguarding?

Cassidy couldn't be certain. But it surely was an interesting development.

She wished that was the *only* development she had to think about right now.

But there was a killer running around on this island.

And Cassidy wasn't confident that this guy was done yet.

AFTER A RESTLESS NIGHT OF SLEEP, Abby managed to drag herself out of bed, shower, and throw on her old clothes. She'd head home to change into something fresh before going to work.

Abby had a cleaning job lined up for the day.

She worked as a maid to earn some extra money since running the theater was expensive and relied mostly on generous donations.

Cleaning wasn't really her thing, but the job was worth it if it allowed her to pursue her dreams of acting.

Downstairs, Tali handed Abby a cup of coffee and a muffin. "You just missed Cassidy."

Abby's breath caught. "Did she have any news?"

Tali frowned and shook her head. "No updates. Sorry."

Abby raised her cup to say thank you. "It's okay. We'll talk more later, okay? I've got to run to work now."

"Whatever you need, sweetheart." Tali thrust a brown paper bag into her hands. "Here's a lunch for you."

"That's sweet. Thank you."

"It was the least I could do."

Abby gave Sugar a rub behind the ears before heading toward the door. As soon as she opened it, she collided into something hard and pine-scented.

She gasped as last night's events flooded back to her.

Was the killer here?

She tensed, ready to fight—if not for herself, then for Tali.

Maybe she could use the steaming coffee as a weapon.

Abby started to draw back her arm to toss the drink in the guy's face, but before she could, the figure grasped her arms to steady her. "I didn't mean to scare you. I was about to step inside."

She looked up.

Hunter.

It was just Hunter.

Her shoulders relaxed, and she let out a feeble laugh. Talk about bad timing.

"Great idea." Hunter nodded at her coffee. "But if you're going to use your coffee for self-defense, be sure to squeeze the cup so the lid flies off as you toss it. You want to get the maximum effectiveness."

He grabbed the napkin nestled around her muffin and used it to wipe the side of the cup where a little coffee had dribbled out.

Abby's cheeks heated, though she wasn't sure why. "Good to know. Thanks for the tip."

"Of course. Are you ready to go?"

She stared at him, no idea what he was talking about. "Go where?"

He shrugged. "Wherever you're going."

Abby felt Tali's eyes on her and decided to step the rest of the way outside to avoid having an audience for whatever embarrassing conversation might occur. "I'm going to work."

"Sounds good. I'll drive."

Abby planted her feet on the ground and stared at him. "What are you talking about?"

Hunter tilted his head as if confused by this whole exchange. "I'm your bodyguard."

"Excuse me?" Her voice squeaked out higher.

His expression remained stoic. "I just got the assignment this morning. I'm keeping an eye on you until this killer is caught."

She let out a shaky laugh. "Are you sure you're

okay after being tased last night? Are you feeling confused? I can barely afford my rent, so I *definitely* can't afford a bodyguard."

He shrugged. "I didn't ask any questions. All I know is that I'm your shadow until further notice."

She narrowed her eyes. Who had hired him?

Then she remembered her book club ladies and the gleam in their gazes when they'd mentioned Hunter last night.

Abby glanced over her shoulder through the picture window into the bookstore.

Tali smiled sweetly from behind the coffee bar and flitted her fingers in the air.

Had her friends done this for her? But they couldn't afford to hire Blackout either, could they?

Abby wasn't sure how much the security group charged for assignments, but she could imagine it was pricey. A thousand dollars a day?

She had no earthly idea.

But she couldn't let her friends go into debt like that for her.

Out of curiosity, she glanced in the brown bag Tali had packed for her. Sure enough, two sandwiches were inside, as well as two bags of chips and two apples.

She narrowed her eyes at the realization.

"I don't know what's going on, but I can't

possibly let you do this." Abby stared up at Hunter, silently begging for him to understand.

Hunter rubbed his jaw before letting out a breath. "How about this? I'll shadow you today, and if payment doesn't work out, it's no big deal. I'd feel better knowing you're okay anyway, especially after everything that happened yesterday."

Though she liked the idea of having someone to watch her back, she didn't want to be a charity case. "Certainly, you have more important people to protect. I know you guys work for CEOs and actresses, singers, political figures. I'm a housekeeper who acts on the side. Not exactly a VIP."

"I wouldn't say that. You're just as important—if not more important—than all those other people. Money doesn't define someone's worth."

Abby's cheeks grew warm.

People usually thought she was overly confident. But in her mind, she was still the overweight, self-conscious girl boys passed over. When she lost weight and finally started to get attention from guys, she'd eaten it up. Had felt on top of the world. Like she was finally seen.

That had led to other problems.

But she still had an insecure side that showed itself sometimes.

Like now.

Like whenever she was around Hunter, for that matter.

Besides, struggling to make ends meet was humbling.

She hadn't always been like this. She'd chosen this lifestyle for herself. She'd chosen to follow her passion even though it came with some sacrifices.

She looked up at Hunter and let out a long breath. "If you insist on shadowing me, get ready to be bored. I need to swing by my place really quick, and then I'm cleaning a rental house."

"That's fine."

She tilted her head. "In that case, you can make yourself useful. Are you any good with a vacuum?"

"I might've used one a time or two." A grin spread across his face. "It's like riding a bike, right? You never forget."

———

Hunter insisted on driving his vehicle instead of Abby's.

Only a few months ago, he'd bought a new Ford F-450. It would be entirely more reliable than Abby's sedan.

He'd transferred the cleaning supplies from the back of Abby's car into his truck bed. He had bins to organize everything so none of the bottles should fall over.

His vehicle was the polar opposite of Abby's car —in both condition and upkeep.

But that was okay. Hunter could appreciate people trying to make ends meet. He'd been there before. When he'd first joined the military, the pay hadn't been great. He managed to scrape by.

When he and Stephanie had gotten married, she hadn't loved living on such a tight budget. Her parents had been well off, and she was used to a certain standard.

It had been hard for her to find employment as a teacher as they'd moved often in the early years of their marriage. Since each state had its own licensing requirements, the process had felt burdensome.

As Hunter had worked his way up the ranks, the paychecks had gotten better. Eventually, he'd even become an officer and, thanks to numerous tours of duty and hazardous duty pay, they'd ended up making a nice living together.

Yes, together.

Even though Stephanie hadn't been in the military, Hunter truly believed spouses of military members fought for the country right alongside them. The support they offered was invaluable.

But he'd realized too late just how much Stephanie resented his job.

Abby's voice pulled him from his thoughts as she called out directions to her place.

After a few moments of silence, Abby glanced at him. "You really think I'm a target?"

Hunter swallowed hard as he contemplated how much to say. "It's a possibility."

He glanced at her again and saw the tremble rake through her.

He felt bad for Abby. He really did.

But hopefully, this would all be wrapped up soon.

They reached her house, and he pulled into the driveway. The place was small, located on the sound side of the island. The outside had seen better days, and the blue paint could use a refresher. Hunter had a feeling she was renting the place.

"I had a nicer place—a duplex. But it burned down at Christmastime."

"I think I remember hearing about that." He most definitely remembered, but he didn't want to sound like he knew too much. He'd heard it had been arson.

But he wouldn't bring that up. She had enough on her plate right now without that memory.

"Housing is difficult to find here on the island. With the price of vacation homes and rentals, every-thing is so expensive."

"I can only imagine." He was grateful he had housing at the Blackout headquarters.

"Anyway," she grabbed the door handle, "I'll just be a minute. I need to change clothes and grab my work smock."

Hunter cut the engine. "I'm going inside with you."

Abby stared at him, and he wondered if she might be annoyed. But the next instant, she nodded, and he followed her up eight steps to the front door.

She shoved the key into the lock and pushed the door open.

Before Abby could step inside, she gasped.

Alarm rushed through him, and Hunter pushed himself in front of her.

As her place came into view, he realized her house had been completely ransacked.

CHAPTER
EIGHT

ABBY STARED at her house in disbelief.

Why would someone do this?

Hunter had already called the police. As soon as he put his phone away, he turned toward her.

"Stay here," he muttered.

Then he withdrew his gun and stepped inside.

Abby watched as Hunter skirted around the items on the floor. His back looked rigid and his muscles tight as if he were braced for trouble.

She remembered how he'd been hit with a Taser last night, and she prayed that didn't happen again. She prayed the killer wasn't hiding inside waiting to strike.

Abby shivered at that thought and glanced around. Not only did she not want Hunter to be hurt but . . . if that happened, she'd be on her own. What would she do?

The neighbors on the left side of her had gone to Florida for the month to see their grandkids. The neighbor on the other side of her was at his second home in Tennessee.

A man named Jimmy James Gamble lived two doors down. He owned a charter boat business with his fiancée, Kenzie. Abby had enjoyed talking to them on occasion.

Jimmy James would be her best bet—if he was home.

Abby released her breath when Hunter finally reappeared and jammed his gun back in his holster. "It's clear."

Even more relief filled her. "Was anything stolen?"

"You're going to have to tell me that." Hunter glanced at her living room. "But it may take a while to figure that out, and we don't want to disturb any evidence. So let's just wait until Cassidy and the gang get here before we do anything."

Abby nodded, knowing his words were wise. They didn't want to jump the gun and somehow ruin the investigation.

Finally, Cassidy and Officer Dane Bradshaw arrived.

Just as Hunter had predicted, they checked things out inside first. Then they asked several questions before finally letting Abby see if anything was missing.

The truth was she didn't have anything of value. Even the laptop she owned was eight years old. She'd bought it used after the fire at her place back in December, and it had been cheap, slow, and unreliable.

She'd sold her jewelry before she moved to Lantern Beach so she could use the funds to put a security deposit on her rental house. Even if she hadn't, she probably would have lost all of it in the fire.

Still, she shouldn't complain.

She was alive.

Unlike Raef.

She frowned.

All morning, she'd been thinking about what she'd tell the cast and crew about him.

They were meeting tonight.

Word had probably already spread through the town, so most of them had probably heard about Raef's murder.

Her other concern—she glanced at her watch—was that she'd be late for work. It seemed small and unimportant compared to what happened to Raef. She knew that.

But she needed this job—if she wanted to stay here on Lantern Beach and get this theater off the ground.

She repressed a sigh.

When would something finally start going right in her life? Because it seemed as if bad luck and tragedy were following her every step she took.

———

An hour later, Hunter and Abby pulled up to a massive oceanside rental house.

Hunter could tell she was anxious. But he wasn't sure if it was simply from the break-in or if there was more to it.

If he knew her better, he might place a hand on her shoulder and remind her to breathe deeply.

But they didn't know each other that well, so he kept his hands to himself.

Now donning a black smock with her name on it, she deposited her cleaning supplies in the elaborate foyer and looked around, a new somberness about her.

"Are you good?" Hunter asked.

She shrugged. "I guess. I just need to have this

cleaned by two o'clock so the new guests can check in. I can't afford to lose this job." She shrugged again as she glanced at him. "I guess you could say I'm living from paycheck to paycheck."

"A lot of artists do that when they're pursuing their dreams."

"Believe it or not, I used to have an office job that paid six figures."

His eyebrows shot up. "Really?"

"Really. And I hated every moment of it. I realized that life was too short to do something I despised. I'd rather live on less but find enjoyment in life than to work a job I hate and count down the moments to the end of each day."

"I get that. You ever regret that choice?"

Abby thought about her answer a moment. "No, not really. Don't get me wrong—I've hit some tough times. There were moments when I knew life would be so much easier if I'd just stuck with doing what was reliable and safe. But life isn't always meant to be safe, you know?"

"I do." Understanding stretched through his voice.

She let out another sigh and glanced around again. "Okay, I need to get to work. Not only do I need to finish cleaning this place by two, but I need to go back to the theater and straighten that up before six."

"What's the hurry at the theater?"

"I have a meeting tonight with the cast and crew, and I need to talk to them about Raef. I need to see if anyone can step into his shoes as the sound tech for the show. We open in six weeks, and we don't have much time to train somebody new."

He grabbed the vacuum. "Just tell me where, and I'll start cleaning the floors."

"I was only joking when I said that."

"You need a hand, and I'm here. I'm not going to just stand by and watch you clean, especially if you're on a time crunch."

Gratitude flashed in her gaze. "I appreciate that. Thank you."

As she doled out directions, Hunter realized he may have been wrong about her.

Abby wasn't as much about fluff and being in the limelight as he'd thought when he first met her.

No, she had a lot of grit and determination.

He could admire that.

But right now, instead of admiring her attributes, Hunter needed to keep his eyes wide open to make sure she remained safe.

HUNTER HAD SURPRISED ABBY.

He'd worked alongside her all morning without complaint. He was mostly quiet, but Abby easily filled the silence with stories. Stories about different houses she'd cleaned and the mishaps she'd experienced.

She'd shared about how some college kids had once filled the entire first floor of a rental with sand when the weather had been too bad to enjoy the beach. Or the family that rearranged every piece of furniture in the house, which took hours to put back in place. Or the guest who'd still been at the house when Abby arrived, who'd complained that the advertisement said the house had "brilliant sunsets." He hadn't seen any during his stay, even though they were promised, and now he wanted his money back.

The three-story house was overwhelming to clean, and it was usually only Abby working there. Having Hunter help made the job go more quickly and took some of the load off of her.

Amazingly enough, at two o'clock, Abby and Hunter finished.

Right on time.

That left Abby four hours to get herself cleaned up, head to the theater to get things in order there, and to gather her thoughts about what she'd say to the cast and crew.

After gathering her supplies and stepping outside, Abby turned to Hunter. "I need to go back to my place to do a few things. Do you think it's okay for me to go in yet?"

"You should call Cassidy to be sure."

She found the police chief's number and gave her a call. Cassidy cleared her to go inside and let her know they hadn't found any additional evidence.

A few minutes later, they were in Hunter's truck headed toward her house again.

"Are you nervous?" He stole a glance at her.

Abby almost denied it but then nodded instead. "I am. I don't know what to tell everybody."

"You'll do great."

Something about the reassurance in his voice bolstered her confidence.

She *could* do this. It wouldn't be fun, but she was the leader of this troupe.

As the woman in charge, she'd make sure Raef got the proper respect he deserved, and she would reassure everyone working with her that things would be okay.

But a lingering question remained in Abby's mind . . . *would* everything truly be okay?

Hunter checked out Abby's house before clearing her to go inside.

The place was still a wreck, and he saw the distress on her face as she surveyed her once-cozy home. At least, it was safe.

"Why don't you take a shower and get cleaned up?" he suggested. "I'll start putting things back in place around here—at least, the things that are obvious."

"You don't have to do that," Abby said.

Yet Hunter *did* feel like he needed to do it. He wanted to help Abby get through this.

"It's no problem," he insisted.

Finally, she nodded. "Thank you."

With one more hesitant glance at him, Abby slipped down the hallway into her bedroom.

As Hunter scanned the house, disgust roiled inside him.

How could someone do something like this? And why?

If they weren't looking for something, then they wanted to send a message. A very clear message.

A message that Abby was next.

Tension roiled inside him at the thought.

Casting those thoughts aside, he started in the kitchen by putting away any unbroken plates or glasses. He swept up some smashed pieces and dumped them in the trashcan. Then he straightened pictures on the walls, readjusted the pillows on the couch, and picked up an overturned plant.

Finally, he stopped at the bookcase in her living room.

The novels and photo albums Abby kept there had been tossed all over the floor.

He wasn't sure what order she liked to keep them, so Abby would have to figure that out later. But for now, he placed them back on the shelves.

He couldn't help but glance through some of the photo albums as he worked.

Many of them featured Abby at her shows. In each one, she was smiling and effervescent.

Effervescent. That was the perfect word to describe her.

Stephanie had been extroverted, but she was different than Abby. She'd sought out attention, mostly because she needed it to feel valued.

Hunter's attention obviously hadn't been enough. Or maybe he'd simply been deployed too much. He still wasn't sure.

Either way, it had been a long time since Hunter had met someone with as much life inside as Abby. Hunter knew Abby was the type who attracted people because of her warm personality and genuine concern.

He wondered about her story. Wondered why she'd come to Lantern Beach of all places. The island was small, not exactly the type of town where most struggling actresses moved in their quest to make it big.

Unless she didn't want to make it big.

Unless, like many people on the island, she'd essentially come here to hide.

Hunter's gut tightened at the thought.

He stuffed the album back on the shelf and then moved onto the next one, knowing time was running out.

But as he picked it up, some photos slid to the floor from between the pages.

Many of them were head shots of Abby.

Several had been torn in half.

His muscles bristled with tension.

Was *this* why this person had broken in? To find pictures of Abby and destroy them? To send her a threatening message?

Hunter wasn't sure, but that was his best guess.

His muscles pulled even tighter.

Abby was definitely a target here, and he didn't like the implications of that.

CHAPTER
TEN

ABBY FELT BETTER after she'd showered and put on some clean clothes.

But as soon as she walked into her living room—which looked amazingly clean—she saw Hunter's face and knew something was wrong.

Cold fear trickled down her spine again.

"What is it?" Her voice sounded strained.

She strode across the room and sat beside him on the couch as she waited for him to begin.

He nodded toward the coffee table. "I found those in your photo album."

Abby glanced at the pictures—the torn photos of herself—and sucked in a breath.

"Why would someone do that?" she finally whispered.

"That's what we need to figure out."

"We need to call Cassidy again." Abby started to grab her phone when Hunter's hand covered her arm.

A jolt of electricity rushed through her, and she quickly pulled away. She could *not* show any signs to indicate just how attracted she was to this man. That would only make this arrangement more awkward since Hunter clearly wasn't interested in her.

"I already called Cassidy," he explained. "I'm going to put those pictures in a bag and take them to the theater. She's going to send someone there to pick them up. She'll check to see if there are any prints on them, though I doubt there are."

"Why do you doubt that?"

"Because this guy didn't leave any other evidence behind. My gut says he's being very careful." Hunter shrugged. "Maybe something will be there. But I wouldn't count on it."

Abby nodded, almost feeling numb at this latest update. "What's this all about?"

"Someone's sending you a message."

"What kind of message?"

Hunter's gaze locked with hers. "That he's not done yet."

The blood drained from her face. This was a nightmare.

But Hunter was right. She was somehow connected with this crime.

Her throat tightened.

"What have I ever done that would make someone do this?" The question left her lips as a whisper.

"It's hard to tell without more evidence."

Abby buried her face in her hands as panic tried to claim her. "What a nightmare."

Surprise washed through her when Hunter placed his hand on her back.

"I know it's a nightmare, but Cassidy is working on this," he murmured. "Maybe we could talk about a few suspects since I'm going to be hanging around for a while."

She lowered her hands from her face as her eyes brightened. "Okay. Right. We can be proactive. But . . . I wouldn't even know where to begin."

"Raef was your sound guy, so you saw him at the theater a lot, right? When you were talking to him, did he ever mention having any arguments with anyone?"

Abby searched her thoughts before shrugging. "His roommate, I suppose."

"Who's his roommate? What did they argue about?"

"His roommate was Peter . . . I don't remember

his last name. But he moved here to work as an electrician, I believe. They were just rooming together as a temporary thing until they could both find their own places. But they were as different as night and day, so it's no surprise they didn't get along."

"Define 'didn't get along.'"

"You know how it goes . . . as far as keeping the house clean and being noisy late at night—Raef liked to stay up late, and Peter went to bed early. I don't think it was anything any more serious than that, though."

"Okay. Anyone else that Raef had a beef with? Anyone involved with the play maybe?"

Abby frowned. "Probably. I mean, Raef wasn't always easy to get along with. He had a big personality, lots of opinions, and he was a talker."

"Can you remember anything specific happening at the theater?"

She nibbled on her bottom lip in thought before letting out a sigh. "There are only two people I can think of who really didn't like him—and I'm not saying either of these people killed him. I mean, I like both of them so . . ."

"No one is going to think you're accusing them. This conversation stays between you and me."

After another moment of hesitation, Abby finally

said, "Devin Turner and Bruno Williams. Devin is the stage manager and Bruno is the lead in the play."

"What was their beef with Raef?"

"I heard Devin badmouthing Raef on more than one occasion. Devin resented the fact that Raef always gave his opinions on things—and Devin got fed up with him. I constantly had to ask Raef to stop talking because our meetings took twice as long when he was there giving his view."

"And Bruno?"

"He thought Raef was doing a terrible job with the sound. Said he made him sound bad on purpose."

"Is that possible?"

She nodded. "You can adjust the treble and the bass, and it will totally change how a person sounds, unfortunately."

"Why would Raef want to make him sound bad?"

"Probably because Raef auditioned for his role but didn't get it. He just didn't have the acting chops for it, and he didn't take it well when he didn't get the part. In fact, not only did he *not* get that particular role, he didn't get *any* role."

"How did he handle that?"

"Not well. I told him we really needed someone with his skills to do the sound. That seemed to give him an ego boost, and he accepted the position. Now

I'm wondering if it would have been better if I just told him no, that we couldn't use him at the theater." Her voice cracked. "Maybe he'd still be alive right now."

Hunter cast her a sympathetic glance. "It's not your fault, you know."

Her throat burned. "Maybe not. But it feels like it is."

A moment of silence stretched between them as Abby fought to regain control of her emotions.

Finally, she glanced at the time and sighed. "I've got to get to the theater to clean up some of the mess before people get there. Seeing any evidence of Raef's death will only add to the shock."

Hunter rose. "Let's go."

Hunter had scrubbed the paint from the floor while Abby took down the police tape.

By the time they finished, the cast and crew began to arrive.

Hunter stood watch as Abby mingled, giving everyone hugs while muttering reassuring words.

She really was good at what she did—dare he say Abby was a far better leader than she gave herself credit for.

As people continued to file in, Hunter took note of everything happening. Cassidy also slipped inside and stood at the back of the room.

He knew why.

Because there was a good chance that someone here could be the killer.

He knew Abby would deny it, that she didn't want to think anyone she had a personal affiliation with might have killed somebody.

But the fact was the killer had gotten into the theater, which indicated he might have some knowledge of this place. The killer possibly had a relationship of some sort with Raef—even if it was only in a professional sense. And the crime had taken place in Abby's office.

That was why he especially wanted to remain on guard right now.

At this point, any number of things could happen.

Finally, a few minutes past six o'clock, Abby stood in front of the stage to address everyone. Tears filled her eyes as she recounted what had happened to Raef.

But Hunter barely heard her words. Instead, he watched the crowd.

He picked out both Devin and Bruno.

Devin was a tall, painfully thin guy in his mid-twenties. Hunter thought he recognized him from a bait and tackle store on the island, which wouldn't surprise him. Most of the actors and crew were volunteers who had other jobs.

Bruno was probably six feet tall and two hundred pounds, much of his weight in his brawny shoulders. Based on the way he smiled at all the women around him, he loved attention, which was probably why he liked acting.

Could either of them be killers?

He couldn't say for sure, but he wanted to keep an eye on them—as well as look for anyone else who might seem off.

But as Abby spoke, no one acted particularly suspicious. Instead, the meeting was filled with tears and some mourning.

Finally, Abby wrapped her talk up. "I hate to say the show must go on, but I'd like to continue with practice. This play means a lot of things to a lot of people. We've all put our blood, sweat, and tears into it. Raef would want us to continue. I truly believe that."

Everyone nodded.

"All right, then, everyone in place. We're going to start rehearsal in five."

Hunter prayed tonight's practice ran smoothly, without any more incidents.

But he could sense that danger was close.

CHAPTER
ELEVEN

ABBY SUCKED in a few calming breaths after talking to the cast and crew members.

She paused near the stage to collect herself before rehearsals began.

She was pleased with how tonight's meeting had gone. She'd prayed God would guide her words, and she felt as if He did.

But part of her felt cold and uncaring to go on with practice, considering what had happened. But that was what Raef would have wanted.

Her gaze wandered to Cassidy, who stood in the back of the theater. She'd seen Hunter talking to her earlier and giving her those photos. But Cassidy had been in no hurry to leave.

Was she here to offer extra security? Or had something else happened?

Abby's pulse pounded harder at that thought.

Hunter made his way toward her as she lingered in front of the stage.

Her throat went dry at the sight of him.

He was so handsome in his light-blue Henley and well-worn jeans. His dark hair and beard . . . well, the guy had practically stepped out of her dreams and into reality.

It was too bad she'd marked off dating.

And that Hunter had marked her off.

Really, there was no possibility that the two of them would ever be together. So Abby needed to stop having these strong reactions to him.

He was simply her bodyguard—at least, he was for the rest of the day.

Tomorrow, Abby would have to figure out a way to convince the book club to fire him and save their money.

He paused in front of her. "Good job tonight."

Just as earlier, his compliment somehow made her flush. It wasn't that Abby never got compliments. But something about hearing those affirming words from Hunter made her heart swell with emotion.

She pushed aside those thoughts to focus on more important matters. "Why is Cassidy still here?"

"Probably just as a precaution."

Abby let out a long breath. "Of course. Since she's here, does that mean that it's quitting time for you?"

He shrugged. "Does danger have a schedule?"

Despite the circumstances, Abby let out a soft laugh. "You do have a sense of humor—even if it is a bit morbid."

He shrugged again. "What can I say?"

Maybe there was a lot about Hunter Bancroft hiding beneath the surface.

Abby wouldn't doubt that was true.

She wanted to uncover it all, to unwrap those layers piece by piece until she figured out who he really was.

But those thoughts were dangerous, and she needed to set them aside for now.

Someone cleared their throat behind her, and Abby turned. Devin stood there, his gaze shifting almost nervously.

"Is everything okay?" Abby instantly sensed that something was wrong.

"I just wanted to let you know that I . . . uh, I . . . let Raef borrow my key to the theater." He rubbed his neck. "Now I see that it was a terrible idea."

"Why did you let him borrow your key?" Hunter asked.

Devin shrugged. "He wanted to surprise you by coming in and getting some things done, by taking some things off your plate. It didn't seem like a big deal at the time. I didn't know . . ." He shrugged again.

"Did you tell Chief Chambers?"

He nodded. "I did."

Abby's thoughts raced. So Raef must have come inside the theater that night. Maybe he hadn't locked the door behind him. Then the killer followed him inside and . . .

She pressed her eyes shut, not wanting to imagine the rest.

Just as she opened her eyes again, a loud crash filled the air.

Her gaze swerved toward the back of the building.

Cassidy dove to the floor as the theater shook and the back wall crumbled.

Abby gasped as she tried to comprehend what had just happened.

———

"Stay here!" Hunter ordered everyone.

He darted toward the back of the building.

He knelt beside Cassidy as she lay still and quickly surveyed her for injuries. "Are you okay?"

She nodded as she pulled herself up, blood trickling from her temple and powdery dust covering her hair. "Yeah, I think so."

Hunter helped her to her feet and then they ran out the back door together.

They paused before they even took three steps.

A car had crashed into the corner of the building.

Cassidy stared at the sedan.

"It's Abby's." Hunter glanced around, but he didn't see the driver fleeing.

Strange.

He walked toward the vehicle and peered inside.

A stick had been jimmied against the accelerator.

Anger burned inside him.

Someone had stolen her car and apparently hot-wired the engine. Then this person had set this whole fiasco up, purposely trying to ram Abby's car into the building.

But why?

Thankfully, the old structure was stronger than it appeared. Otherwise, they could have casualties right now.

"What if this has all been a distraction?" he muttered aloud.

He and Cassidy exchanged a look before rushing back inside.

They paused. Most of the cast and crew were on

the stage looking bewildered. Hunter's gaze searched the crowd until he found Abby.

She had her arms around two of the younger cast members as she stared at him, almost as if waiting for an update or reassurance.

He nodded at her and let out a breath, grateful that she was okay.

"What can I help you do?" he asked Cassidy.

"Let's get everyone down here sitting together so I can get statements. Meanwhile, I'll get the rest of my crew out here so they can investigate." Her gaze locked with his. "I don't like what's happening around here."

Neither did he, Hunter mused. Neither did he.

CHAPTER
TWELVE

ABBY FELT her fear growing as she sat in the front row of the theater.

The rest of the cast and crew were also seated and murmuring amongst themselves. The smell of dust and debris lingered in the air, along with a cool breeze from where the wooden wall had been cracked open.

The killer's behavior was escalating.

Now it appeared she wasn't the only one in danger. Anyone around her could be collateral damage in a killer's rampage.

She shivered again. The other officers had arrived on the scene and were investigating both outside and inside. Abby felt better knowing they were here.

Hunter lingered close, and Cassidy's husband, Ty, had also shown up.

Finally, thirty minutes after law enforcement had arrived, Abby rose. She needed an update, and she couldn't just sit here any longer.

She paced down the aisle toward Cassidy.

As soon as Cassidy saw her, she put her hand on Abby's shoulder. "How are you holding up?"

Abby shook her head. "I'm devastated. What's going on?"

"Whoever did this with your car is long gone. He shoved that stick on the accelerator and then took off, probably in his own vehicle. We're asking around, of course, to see if anyone saw anything. But so far, we don't have any witnesses."

Abby bit down. Of course they didn't.

Whoever this was knew what they were doing.

Cassidy studied Abby's face a moment. "Have you thought of anything else that might help us?"

She shook her head. "I wish I had something to offer you, but I don't. Do you not have any leads at this point?"

Cassidy glanced around as if there was something she wanted to say but couldn't, probably for confidentiality reasons. "We're looking at someone from Raef's work whom he had an argument with. Plus, he and his roommate have been having some conflicts. Did he ever tell you anything about either of those situations?"

Abby shook her head. "It probably seems as if we were close. We weren't. I wish I could help you more. I wish I could tell you more information. But even when the two of us went to dinner yesterday, we didn't talk about any problems, per se. We talked about theater and places that we'd been in the past and food. It was very surface level."

Cassidy nodded. "I understand."

Abby glanced back at the theater wall and frowned. "What does this mean? I can only assume the building isn't safe anymore?"

Cassidy followed her gaze. "It doesn't look good, unfortunately. I'll have the building inspector come out to check the structural damage, but I can't imagine this will be an easy fix."

Discouragement pressed down on Abby. "Is my cast and crew free to leave?"

Cassidy nodded. "We talked to everyone we needed to speak to. So go ahead and send them home. I hope to have an update for you in the morning. I'm sure you're anxious to know how to plan."

"You could say that." Her lips tugged downward into a deeper frown.

Cassidy's gaze locked with Abby's, the look in her eyes dead serious. "In the meantime, be careful, please."

Abby nodded. Cassidy wouldn't have to tell her twice.

Tali offered to let Abby sleep at her apartment again tonight, so Hunter drove her there from the theater and walked her inside. He needed to take every precaution possible.

Mac greeted Hunter at the door. "Why don't you head home for tonight? I'll be here, and I can keep an eye on things."

He cast a glance at Abby, still hesitant to leave her.

"You should go and get your rest," Mac continued. "I'm not sure if you'll be on the job again tomorrow, but if you are you'll need some sleep tonight."

"I'll be fine." Abby gave him a pointed look. "Plus, you've already done so much for me."

Then why did Hunter feel like he hadn't done enough? However, it wasn't as if he could have anticipated a car slamming into the theater. He was so thankful no one had been hurt.

Still, he wanted to talk to Abby.

The two hadn't been able to chat on the way here since she'd been on the phone with her insurance company about the theater and her car.

"I'll go home tonight and be back in the morning." Hunter knew that was only wise—although part of him was tempted to sleep on one of the couches at the coffee house just to be on the safe side. "Can I have a moment with you before I go, though?" He glanced at Tali and Mac. "Alone?"

"Of course." Tali took Mac's arm and led him upstairs.

Then Hunter turned to Abby, noting her widening eyes as she looked up at him.

Hunter wasn't sure why he had the unexplainable urge to take care of her. To help find her a new car. To reassure her that everything would be okay.

They didn't have that kind of relationship.

Instead, he stuffed his hands deep into his pockets as he observed Abby a moment. "Are you sure you're okay?"

She nodded and pushed a dark lock of hair behind her ear. "As well as I can be. I still have a lot to figure out."

"What's on your schedule tomorrow?"

"Tomorrow? I have two houses to clean—smaller ones this time. I'll probably have more things to do regarding insurance for the theater and my car. Hopefully, I'll hear back from the building inspector about whether or not the theater can remain open. I have a feeling I know what that answer will be, however." Her voice faded with discouragement.

He bit back a frown. Hunter knew it didn't look good.

But he hoped for Abby's sake that something began working in her favor.

CHAPTER
THIRTEEN

CASSIDY WAS EXHAUSTED by the time she got home from work that evening.

Ty had already picked up Faith, their fifteen-month-old daughter, from his parents' house next door. She was asleep and safely tucked in her bed.

Though Cassidy was grateful she could relax, she missed the routine of holding her daughter and then putting her into bed.

But sometimes her job demanded long hours. Thankfully, Ty generally had flexibility with his job, and his parents were close and loved to help. Teamwork was the only way Cassidy could make being a working mom successful. But it wasn't for the faint of heart.

Cassidy changed into some comfortable joggers

and a sweatshirt, and then she and Ty sat on the couch to unwind before bed.

A question had been lingering in her mind all day, but she hadn't had a chance to talk to Ty about it yet.

She turned toward her husband, who looked comfortable in his black sweats and white T-shirt. His light-brown hair was tousled, and his blue eyes still looked surprisingly alert considering how much they'd both had going on lately. Ty was getting ready for another round of guests coming to Hope House, the nonprofit he'd started to help those struggling after their military service ended.

Seeing him still made her heart flutter. She hoped that never changed.

"Something on your mind?" He raised his eyebrows.

"As a matter of fact, yes." Cassidy tucked her feet beneath her. "I know what Blackout's rates are. How in the world are Tali, Serena, and Cadence able to afford to hire Hunter to guard Abby? I know it's none of my business, but I just can't make sense of it."

Ty shrugged as if her question didn't surprise him. "The ladies said they'd take a loan out if they had to."

"What?" Cassidy's voice came out louder than

she intended, and she quickly lowered it before she woke up Faith. "That's ridiculous."

"Don't worry." Ty shrugged again, still appearing unbothered. "We'll work something out for them. You know we like to take care of our own."

Cassidy tilted her head at his words. "Abby falls into that category?"

"She's a friend of Mac's, and that makes her a friend of ours."

Cassidy smiled. She'd always loved how giving and generous Ty was. His kindness was just one more reason to admire him—but she already had a long list, and she counted herself fortunate to be married to him.

She felt better knowing that Tali and the gang wouldn't go into massive debt just to keep their friend safe.

Ty shifted and stretched his arm across the back of the couch. "So, what's going on with your investigation? Any leads?"

Cassidy let out a slow sigh as the case trickled back into her mind. Not that she'd been able to forget about it. On a small island like Lantern Beach, any type of crime made people nervous. Locals were already talking, telling neighbors to lock their doors and not go anywhere alone.

"Few and far between," she finally said. "No one

seems to have the magic trio of motive, means, and opportunity."

"Who are you looking at?"

She let out another breath as she thought through her suspects. "First of all, there's Jeremiah Chen. He worked with Raef at Ocean Essence, and the two of them had a blowout only two days before Raef was murdered. But really, the reasoning for their blowout doesn't seem like motive for murder, and he has an alibi for the time Raef died. He was at a friend's house."

"Sounds like you can rule him out. Who else?"

"Peter Jones was Raef's roommate. The two didn't know each other before moving in together, and they apparently didn't get along either. That seems to be a theme for Raef. The only reason I'm still looking at Jones is because he was arrested two years ago for breaking and entering. He says the whole thing was a misunderstanding, but . . ."

"Most criminals have good excuses lined up."

Cassidy nodded. "Exactly. Then there's another guy in the play I'm keeping my eye on. His name is Bruno Williams. Last week, he got into a fist fight at Waterman's. He'd been drinking too much at the time. Anyway, the guy clearly has a temper. And he, unlike Jeremiah, does *not* have an alibi."

"Interesting." Ty nodded slowly. "At least, you have a few suspects."

Cassidy's jaw tightened. "We'll see if they lead anywhere."

She had a feeling this mystery was just beginning to unravel.

She had no idea what else she should expect.

ABBY HADN'T BEEN able to sleep much last night. She had too much on her mind.

Raef's death had only been the beginning of her worries. Add to that everything else that happened, including Hunter being tased, the theater being destroyed, and her car being weaponized.

She'd depleted her savings to open this theater. There was no way she could qualify for a loan right now to make repairs to the building. Insurance might cover most of it, but there would still be money out of her pocket for deductibles.

Then there was her car. How would she get around the island—and to work—without a vehicle?

She could probably buy a bicycle, but it would be difficult to tote around her cleaning supplies on the back of a bike.

Abby had played out various scenarios in her head as she'd lain in bed until finally she couldn't lie still any longer. She was determined to be independent. To be different than her own mother.

She thought she'd done everything right, but life had other plans, apparently.

As she rose, she tried to remain quiet, especially since it was only 6:30. But when she emerged from her room, Tali and Mac were already seated at the kitchen table.

They called good morning and waved her over. Mac pulled out a chair for her, and Abby plopped into it, still groggy. Sugar, on the other hand, was already a bundle of energy as he wagged his tail and demanded a head rub. Abby obliged.

"You don't look like you slept very well." Tali rose to fix her a cup of coffee.

Abby didn't stop her. It wouldn't have done any good to argue anyway.

"I didn't." Abby didn't bother to try to hold back her frown. But she did offer up a grateful smile immediately afterward when Tali placed the coffee in front of her.

She took several sips, hoping the caffeine would help wake her and clear her thoughts.

"What am I going to do about the theater?" She glanced back and forth between Mac and Tali. She treasured their wisdom and advice, and she could really use both of those things right now. "Will the building even be salvageable?"

They exchanged a look, and Abby had a feeling the two of them had already talked about this.

"That building has been renovated and brought up to code once already," Mac reminded her. "It can be fixed again."

Abby nodded, knowing his words were true, and then she glanced at her phone, waiting to hear back from the building inspector. She knew it was entirely too early for a phone call. But impatience was getting the best of her right now.

Mac seemed to know exactly what she was thinking and said, "You probably won't hear anything until this afternoon at the earliest."

"It takes that long?"

He nodded somberly. "I can try to speed up the process, but it won't do any good. Billy Wallop—the inspector—is very thorough."

"I suppose that's good." Abby frowned. "But the show is supposed to open in six weeks! And I almost forgot, but a reporter from a newspaper in Raleigh is supposed to interview me in two days about the play."

"Maybe you should still do the interview and let everyone know what's happened. It will be a good way to spread the word. Even bad news can be good news when it comes to publicity, right?"

She frowned. "I just wanted everything to stay on track."

"I know, but you have to think about the safety of your cast and crew and guests first." Tali patted her hand as compassion stretched through her voice.

Abby knew her friend's words were true. But she didn't want them to be. She wanted to figure out a way to use the theater, no matter what the results of the building inspection were.

But the thought was selfish. If this play was delayed for some reason, then God had a purpose in it. Maybe He was teaching her another lesson. She'd already been taught a lot. First with boyfriend-turned-creep Nelson Woods back in Florida. Then with fellow castmate Michael LeBlanc in Myrtle Beach, who'd tried to ruin her reputation to save himself.

"For the record, I don't need a bodyguard," Abby announced. "I appreciate how you guys are trying to watch out for me, but—"

"It was Serena's idea," Tali admitted.

"I figured as much." Abby frowned.

"Having Hunter around isn't a bad idea," Mac said. "At least, until we know what's going on. It doesn't mean you're weak—it just means you need someone to watch your back. We all do."

She frowned again. "Controlling men seem to be drawn to me like moths to light. I don't like to be controlled."

"Hunter isn't trying to control you," Mac insisted. "He's just protecting you."

That might be true, but Hunter seemed like the controlling type.

Abby didn't tell Mac about one of the previous times she'd talked to the man. She'd been walking on the beach when a storm rose. She'd run into him, and he'd said—she remembered his exact words—Are you out of your mind being out here right now?

She'd pointed out that he was also outside, but he'd insisted he'd had a good reason.

She found out later that a dead body had washed ashore.

But still . . . his tone made it clear that he was the type who told people what to do.

She took another sip of her coffee before setting the mug back on the table and glancing outside. The sun was beginning to rise over the ocean. It really was a beautiful sight, one she'd never get tired of seeing.

But Abby's thoughts quickly shifted back to the problems pressing on her from every side.

"Meanwhile, Raef's killer is still out there." She frowned again. "That's really what I should be concentrating on and concerned about, not the theater."

"You have a lot of things going on." Tali squeezed her hand.

"Most killers would flee out of fear of being caught," Mac muttered as his eyes narrowed with thought. "Not this guy."

Abby sucked in a breath at his statement. But his words were true.

The guy who'd killed Raef didn't seem to be on the run.

He must not be finished yet.

She shuddered.

He must have quite a motive behind all this.

But what could it be?

Abby's stomach rumbled with turmoil.

Tali threw Mac a warning glance.

"Sorry," Mac muttered with a shrug. "Maybe I shouldn't think aloud. But you're a smart girl, Abby, and you probably already realized what I said was true."

"You're right. Why *won't* this guy leave? Staying here will just make it easier for him to get caught. Unless . . . Raef wasn't his target."

Her statement hung in the air.

She didn't say anything else. Nor did Mac or Tali.

But they all knew the truth.

If Raef wasn't the intended target, that meant . . . Abby was.

Fear washed through her at the thought.

———

Since Hunter didn't need to meet Abby until 8:30, he decided to go on his morning jog. He loved routine, and this was one of his.

Axel accompanied him.

Their normal route involved them leaving the Blackout campus and heading down the gravel road at the northern end of the island. From there, they would pass the church they attended, a few patches of woods, and eventually they'd reach Ty and Cassidy's place.

That was their cue to turn around and head back. Along the way, there were a couple of small bridges with narrow creeks trickling beneath. Overall, it was a beautiful run, but Hunter had been warned that, in the summer, mosquitoes and biting flies would be his enemy.

"Did you hear the news?" Axel asked beside him, an excitement to his voice, as they continued jogging down the gravel road.

"What news?" Hunter asked.

"I finally popped the question last night to Olivia."

Hunter's eyes widened. "What? No way. I heard you were a confirmed bachelor."

"When you know, you know. I've known she's the one for a long time." He grinned.

Axel and Olivia had been dating for a couple of years now. Olivia had started her own marketing firm here on the island, and her calm but confident personality was the perfect complement to Axel's.

Hunter had thought he and Stephanie were perfect together—that opposites attracted. But that had been a big mistake. If he ever did marry again, which he didn't plan on doing, he'd find someone more like him. Someone steadier. More responsible.

"Well, congratulations, man," Hunter said. "I'm really happy for you."

"Thanks. We're pretty excited too."

"When's the big day?"

"We're still hashing that out, but we're thinking sometime in the summer." Axel shrugged. "Olivia wants to get married on the beach, and I think that's a great idea. I think whatever makes her happy is a great idea." He grinned.

"Wise words."

As they continued jogging, Hunter's thoughts

drifted to Stephanie. When he'd met her at a friend's party, he'd thought she was the one also. They'd started dating, and he'd been swept up in a whirlwind.

Hunter hadn't expected to ever lose her. He thought they'd have more time to work out their problems, to overcome their differences. Sadness pressed on him at the memories of what he'd lost.

His thoughts drifted to Abby.

He remembered hearing her laugh last night when he'd made the comment about danger not taking a break.

The sound had been infectious and had made everything around them brighter.

In fact, when she'd stopped laughing, Hunter had found himself craving hearing the sound again.

Which was crazy.

He needed to stop thinking like that.

He needed to think about more practical matters —like her opposition to his protection and how he could convince her to let him protect her longer.

He also knew she was worried about not having a car—and not having money to buy a new one.

He'd asked around at the Blackout headquarters last night and found out Maddox, one of his colleagues, was looking to buy a new vehicle. Hunter had already checked out Maddox's old car, a silver

2013 Honda Civic, and he thought it might work for Abby.

But he wasn't sure if Abby would accept his help. He needed to plan that carefully. The last thing he wanted was for her to think he considered her a charity case. He knew her well enough to know that wouldn't go over well.

Stephanie hadn't wanted to hear his opinion on anything. She'd been offended if he ever offered an alternate view.

The two had definitely had their problems.

But what had she been hiding from him?

As if Axel were reading Hunter's thoughts, Axel said, "I heard you might be buying Maddox's old Civic."

"Word travels, fast, huh?"

"What do you need another car for? I thought you liked your truck." A playful, knowing tone filled Axel's voice.

Hunter knew exactly what his friend was doing—fishing for information.

Hunter sucked in a deep breath. "You know why. Abby's car was totaled, and she has no means of getting around the island. She hasn't said this to me directly—and she probably won't—but I'm nearly certain she doesn't have the money to buy anything else."

"That's nice of you to help her."

Hunter shrugged off his friend's words. "I'm just trying to be a decent human being."

"Sounds like there's something more than what's professional going on between you two." Axel's words contained a teasing undertone.

Hunter let out a brisk—and dismissive—laugh. "Don't be ridiculous."

He didn't miss the look that Axel threw at him. But there was nothing personal going on. Hunter was simply trying to keep Abby safe and to watch out for someone in need.

Wasn't that what he'd been taught in church? To help others?

He'd only started going to church a year ago. He'd gotten lost deep in the despair of his mistakes, and he hadn't thought he'd ever break free.

But when a friend had started talking to him about Jesus, things had started to change. It hadn't been an easy process. Sometimes, Hunter still wanted to fall back into his old ways.

But his life was so much better with his faith in God intact.

Hunter's actions had nothing to do with the fact that he was mildly attracted to Abby.

Well, maybe closer to moderately attracted to her.

Okay . . . *very* attracted to her. She was gorgeous

and sweet. Intelligent and kind. He could see himself enjoying her company for long after this assignment was over . . . except he wouldn't.

Abby was exactly the kind of woman he needed to stay away from. The two would ultimately be like gunpowder and fire—the perfect ingredients for an explosion.

But he'd just been thinking about how faith without works was dead. So he'd decided to watch what was happening around him and pray that God would show him simple ways he could show love to others.

Abby's car problems had practically smacked him in the face.

As Hunter and Axel continued jogging, a noise sounded behind them, snapping Hunter's thoughts back to his surroundings.

He glanced over his shoulder, and his eyes widened.

A car had appeared out of nowhere.

The vehicle loitered behind them.

Until the driver gunned the engine.

And aimed straight for them.

HUNTER AND AXEL dove out of the way.

Hunter hit the marsh grass beside him, and the blades cut into his flesh.

At least, the ground was soft and mushy—not to mention a little damp.

As the car's engine revved again, Hunter glanced at Axel.

His friend appeared okay.

They both rose to their feet and stared at the road.

But it was too late to get the car's plates.

The driver was too far away and too much dust flew behind him.

But from what Hunter could tell, the vehicle was a black Camry.

"I didn't see that one coming," Axel muttered as

they climbed out of the damp, sulfurous-smelling marsh. "You okay?"

Hunter saw the small scrapes on his arms and legs. He felt the pricks on his neck.

But the outcome could have been so much worse.

If he and Axel hadn't jumped out of the way when they did . . .

Hunter's back muscles tightened at the thought.

"I'm fine. You?" Hunter glanced over his friend and saw Axel was in the same boat. He had a lot of small scrapes and cuts on his exposed skin.

But otherwise, he appeared fine.

Still . . . why would someone try to run *them* over? Did this have something to do with a past Blackout assignment?

He didn't think so.

If he had to guess, this had to do with Raef's murder.

All the evidence made it appear that either Raef or Abby were the targets. So what sense did it make for someone to come after Axel or Hunter?

Were they all targets?

Hunter frowned.

He wasn't sure. But a bad feeling brewed in his gut.

———

Abby glanced at her watch again.

Where was Hunter?

It was 8:45. A few more minutes, and she'd be late for her job. Then she wouldn't have time to clean both the houses she had scheduled for today, which would then mean a reduction in her paycheck.

She couldn't afford to lose any pay, considering everything that had happened.

Abby usually tried not to stress over money. Somehow things always seemed to work out, and God always provided—especially when the providing seemed impossible. However, she liked not having to depend on anyone else, to do things on her own merit.

What if that wasn't possible?

But given everything that had happened, Abby's nerves were on edge, and worry pulsed through her.

She glanced at her watch again and frowned.

She'd pegged Hunter as the punctual type. That was why she was so surprised when he hadn't arrived at 8:30 as he'd said he would.

She should fire him. She could do that, right? Though she hadn't officially hired him, this was ridiculous. Yesterday, she should have simply refused.

Mac had volunteered to take her to the jobsite, but Abby insisted she'd give Hunter a few more minutes.

Besides, all her cleaning supplies were in the back of his truck.

Finally, he pulled in front of the shop. As he hopped out and strode toward the door, not appearing in a hurry, her saltiness grew.

"I thought you were going to be here at 8:30?" The accusatory words left her lips before she could stop them.

As soon as they did, Abby regretted it.

Especially when she saw the small cuts on his neck and the side of his face.

Something had happened.

"Are you okay?" Abby instinctually reached toward him and grasped his arm.

She'd always been a touchy-feely girl, but she tried to restrain herself around Hunter because he didn't seem like a touchy-feely guy.

Grabbing him now was just visceral.

Tali and Mac rushed toward them, Sugar at their heels. They'd been chatting at the coffee bar only seconds earlier.

"There was a little accident this morning." Hunter shrugged as if what had happened wasn't a big deal.

"An accident?" Abby's heartbeat quickened as her mind played through the possibilities. "What do you mean an accident?"

His expression remained stoic. "Someone tried to run over Axel and me as we were jogging."

Mac stepped closer, and surprise laced his words as he muttered, "What?"

Hunter rubbed a hand over his beard. "We were able to get out of the way and jump into the marsh. But we didn't get the guy's plates. We called Cassidy, of course, and she put out a BOLO for the vehicle. They already found it."

"They did?" Hope lit Abby's voice. "Even without knowing the plates?"

Hunter nodded. "It wasn't hard to find."

Did that mean Hunter had some answers?

She held her breath as she waited for him to continue.

"The car was stolen from a tourist who'd pulled off the road to take a picture of the sunrise. The thief ended up leaving it at a public beach access lot with no cameras, of course. So we're no closer to finding out the person behind this than we were before."

Disappointment chomped down deep on Abby. That wasn't the news she wanted to start her day with.

She'd been hoping and praying for a better day today. She'd even foolishly thought, how could things get worse?

They clearly could.

She shivered and wrapped her arms across her chest as she glanced around. Trouble suddenly seemed as if it could be hiding around every bend.

Maybe because it was. Now the person who'd been hired to protect her was in danger.

With every new development, she could feel the noose tightening.

Not the killer's noose.

But she was losing control of her life, her schedule, even her reactions it seemed.

She didn't like feeling trapped. Feeling smothered.

"Maybe I should just stay here today." Her voice sounded hoarse as she asked the question. "Maybe I'm better off not going out until this person is behind bars."

That was the last thing she wanted, but she needed to be practical.

Hunter glanced at Mac, a silent conversation passing between them.

"In theory, that might be true," Hunter said. "But what if this guy isn't caught? You can't stay in hiding indefinitely. Then he'll just win. I think you should continue on like normal."

"But with Hunter at your side." Mac cast her a knowing look.

Familiar heat crept up her cheeks.

How long would Hunter be forced to accompany her everywhere? Did he resent this assignment? Was she just another thing to add to his caseload?

He hadn't made her feel like a burden—yet she still did.

How could she be her own person and remain safe?

She frowned. Right now, she couldn't.

Finally, Abby nodded. If she were honest, she'd admit she felt better when he was at her side. "Okay, but I feel like this just got even more personal."

No one argued with her.

That only confirmed that her concern was legit.

HUNTER WAS on guard as he drove toward Abby's job. He didn't want anything else to surprise him.

They pulled up to the first house Abby needed to clean, and he put his truck in Park as he observed the home.

Thankfully, this one was much smaller than the one they'd cleaned yesterday. The place was only one story and probably just over a thousand square feet.

"You ready for this?" Hunter glanced at her.

Abby let out a sigh and nodded. "The sooner I get started, the sooner I get done."

They went inside and started to work. Hunter stayed in the same room with Abby as they cleaned, just to be on the safe side.

But Hunter noticed a new somberness about

Abby as she worked. She wasn't as chatty as usual. He missed her cheerfulness, the positive vibes she always spread to everyone around her.

Stephanie had been social and extroverted also—but in a different way. She'd gotten into the party scene. She liked to drink—and when she did, she made poor decisions. The friends she hung out with only made things worse.

But Hunter hadn't been able to talk any sense into her.

As they finished cleaning the kitchen, someone knocked at the door.

His muscles tensed at the sound.

Abby paused from wiping the counters and glanced at Hunter.

As he stepped toward the door, he withdrew his gun.

Killers didn't usually knock, but he wanted to use the utmost caution right now.

"Stay out of sight, just in case," he muttered.

Abby stared at him with wide eyes, but she nodded and moved toward the wall.

He walked to the door and peered out the peephole.

A woman in her fifties with stringy, thin brown hair stood outside. Hunter noted she wore a black smock similar to Abby's, with a name embroidered on it.

"Do you know a Florence?" he asked Abby.

"Florence? She's my boss." Abby's voice relaxed some, and she stepped out.

"Does she usually stop by when you're cleaning?"

"Sometimes she checks on me. You can let her in."

Hunter slipped his gun back into its holster and then opened the door.

Florence glanced at him in surprise before her gaze found Abby's.

Then she grinned. "I wasn't expecting you to have a friend with you."

Abby glanced at Hunter, but she didn't bother to explain he was more of a bodyguard than a friend.

He was glad. He was starting to like the idea that this could be more than a business arrangement—even though it wasn't. He'd guarded plenty of people before. For some reason, protecting Abby felt different.

He reminded himself to keep his distance. Boring —that was the kind of woman he needed to date. He reminded himself he was all shadows, and Abby was all limelight.

He needed to find someone else who liked remaining in the background also—at least, if he wanted to protect his heart, he did.

"I just wanted to see how things were going," Florence explained as she stepped inside. "I pulled up to the house, and I fully expected to look in the window and see you dancing, and to hear you singing before I even got to the door."

Hunter hid a smile. He could totally see Abby acting out her musicals in order to pass time as she cleaned these houses alone.

But not today.

Today, her smile was fleeting.

And Hunter missed her cheerfulness. He even missed the fake accents he often heard her practicing.

As Abby and Florence talked a few more minutes, Hunter stayed close, just to be safe.

"You know, I'm going to have to tell CJ you're taken," Florence finally said, casting a glance at Hunter.

"Excuse me?" Abby's voice rose with surprise. CJ Falkner was part of the stage crew for the play.

"He's had a terrible crush on you." Florence laughed. "He's my nephew, you know."

"I had no idea you were related—or that he had a crush on me." CJ wasn't exactly her type, with his ruddy complexion and love of all things Dungeons and Dragons. Plus, he was at least five years younger.

"Anyway, with your looks, I'm sure all the boys have crushes on you."

Abby shrugged as if trying to figure out how to gracefully correct the woman's assumption that Abby and Hunter were together. "I don't know if I'd say that."

Florence crossed her arms, clearly ready to shoot the breeze. "Did I tell you that some guy called the office last week asking about you?"

Abby straightened and glanced at Hunter. "Is that right?"

Hunter stepped closer. "What was this person asking about her?"

"Said he was checking your references, that you'd put in an application somewhere else." Florence stared at Abby. "Is that true? I'm already so short-staffed and—"

"I didn't apply anywhere else," Abby quickly interjected.

Florence shook her head, a bewildered expression on her face. "That's so strange. But I did give you a glowing recommendation."

"Did this man say anything else?" Hunter's voice hardened as he slipped into interrogation mode.

"Not really."

"He didn't say what company he was with?" Had

someone simply been fishing for information about her? Hunter didn't like the thought of that.

"If he did, I don't remember." Florence shrugged. "I'm sorry. I wish I could tell you more, but that's all I can recall. The conversation seemed pretty mundane—other than the fact that I thought I might be losing one of my more reliable employees."

"I assure you that I'm not going anywhere."

Florence's eyes sparkled. "That's good. Because the business might be getting a revamp soon. I'll tell you more details as soon as I can. Now, I've really got to run and check on my other houses."

Hunter couldn't get the conversation out of his mind after Florence left.

He didn't say anything, but he was sure that he and Abby were thinking the same thing.

Had it been the killer who'd contacted Florence? But why would he do that? What purpose would it serve?

After a few moments of silence, Abby's phone buzzed, and she glanced at it with a frown. Tension rolled across her expression.

"It's the building inspector," she murmured.

"No need to delay the inevitable."

Her frown deepened, but she nodded. As she answered, putting the phone on speaker, her voice tightened. "This is Abby."

Billy Wallop came over the line. "Ms. Mendez, I'm sorry to tell you this, but I'm going to have to condemn the theater. It's not safe for anyone to be inside. Not you, not the cast and crew, and definitely not any guests. As of this moment, the place is off-limits."

Tears flooded Abby's eyes. She asked Billy a few more questions and then thanked him before ending the call. As soon as her phone was in her pocket, she leaned against the wall with her shoulders slumped in defeat.

More than anything, Hunter wanted to pull Abby into an embrace and tell her everything would be okay.

The pain in her eyes was positively heartbreaking.

But he kept his distance, remembering the professional standards he had in place.

Abby didn't want to believe Billy's update. She'd been praying for better news. Hoping against hope that maybe her car hadn't done as much damage to the theater as she thought.

But she'd been wrong.

Was it even possible to make a condemned building usable again? She thought the structure could be repaired. But how much money would that take?

More than she had.

Her chest tightened.

Abby would have to give up her dream of living here, wouldn't she? Go back to her old job, which had made her miserable, but at least it had brought in a reliable paycheck.

Maybe coming here and starting this theater troupe had been foolish.

Maybe she should have never come to Lantern Beach. It had been a leap of faith—and a mistake.

She'd risked everything—and now, everything was gone.

Hunter stepped closer and squeezed her arm. "Hey, it's going to be okay."

She tried to hold back her tears. She hadn't expected the waterworks to come on so strong. She was usually such an optimist.

But Abby couldn't deny the reality in front of her any longer.

Her situation was grim on more than one front. She didn't want to follow in her mom's footsteps. Her mom had tried to follow her dreams but, in the end, she'd failed. As a result, Abby had moved from place to place. Her mom had moved in with man after man.

Her mom had been unable to survive on her own.

She'd died of a drug overdose when Abby was twenty-one.

Abby was determined not to let that be her own fate. It was one of the reasons she stayed far away from drugs, alcohol, and partying.

And controlling men—though she'd apparently failed at that one. Instead, she'd dated men who hadn't initially seemed controlling. Yet, when they showed their true colors, they were.

At least, Hunter didn't try to hide his tendencies.

"Look." Hunter stepped even closer. "We got a lot done here today, and we got it done fast. How about if we grab some lunch at The Crazy Chefette? My treat. I feel like you need to have a breather from all this, and maybe having a good meal will do that."

Abby glanced at him, grateful for his concern and thoughtfulness. His compassion surprised her. Maybe he wasn't such an ogre after all.

Then she nodded. "That sounds good."

They gathered the cleaning supplies and took them out to the truck. She noticed Hunter glancing around with every move they made.

He wasn't taking any chances, was he? Abby didn't complain. His attention to detail made her feel safe.

A few minutes later, they pulled up to The Crazy Chefette.

Cadence seated them right away and didn't even have to take their orders. "The usual, coming right up."

Apparently, they were both frequent enough guests that she knew exactly what they wanted.

"I didn't take you to be a creature of habit." Hunter gazed at her from across the table.

He'd made sure to sit where he could see the front door, a fact that hadn't gone unnoticed by Abby.

"Food is my comfort."

"That's surprising."

She frowned before admitting, "I used to be overweight, actually. My home life was turbulent growing up, to say the least, and food always made me feel better. Especially potato chips. By the time I hit sixteen, I despised my own body."

Hunter waited quietly for her to continue.

"I went to an amusement park with my class at school, but when I got on one of the rollercoasters, I didn't fit. They asked me to get off." Her cheeks heated. "My classmates were nearby and heard. They began laughing uncontrollably. It was humiliating, to say the least."

"I'm sorry. Kids can be cruel."

"After that, I decided to make some changes. I

started exercising and lost the weight. I basically turned my life around. I turned a lot of the attention I'd given to food over to acting instead."

"It takes a lot of self-control to lose weight. Good job." Hunter's voice held no judgment.

Some people did look at her differently after Abby told them she used to be overweight.

She wasn't sure why she wanted to put that on the table, but she did. She didn't want to hide with shame from her past and her mistakes. In fact, she found it helpful to be real with people. Sometimes people needed to see that others' lives weren't picture perfect.

Hunter, on the other hand, probably couldn't understand. He seemed about as perfect as they came.

Her thoughts shifted from her admission about the past to her new reality in the present.

Her smile slipped again. "Until I can figure out what's going on, we're going to shut down rehearsals. I'm going to need to tell the cast and crew this update. However, I clearly can't meet with them in the theater as I usually do."

"I bet if you talk to Pastor Jack, he'd let you use the church for the meeting. Otherwise, you could see if you could use the school."

Abby nodded. "That's a good idea. I'll talk to Pastor Jack."

Before they could chat anymore, someone paused by their table.

Abby glanced up at the dark-haired Asian man with terse movements. He looked vaguely familiar, like someone she may have seen around on the island before.

"I didn't do it," he rushed as sweat spread across his forehead.

Abby's eyes widened. "Didn't do what?"

"I didn't kill Raef." His words came out fast. "I know that's what you're thinking, but it's not true."

Abby glanced at Hunter and saw him bristle.

Hunter shifted as he stared at the man before shaking his head. "I'm sorry, but . . . who are you?"

HUNTER STARED AT THE MAN, already feeling uneasy.

"I'm Jeremiah, and I worked with Raef at the lab," he explained. "The police chief came in and questioned me, and now I'm pretty certain everyone thinks I killed him. I would never do that."

Surprise washed through Hunter at the man's explanation. "Why would they think you did it?"

"Just because we got into that argument at work, it doesn't mean anything." Jeremiah sliced his hand through the air.

"What kind of argument?" Abby glanced at Hunter, a wrinkle of confusion on her forehead.

"Raef was deep-cleaning a microscope in the lab when he slipped. His elbow hit the beaker I was working with, and the chemicals inside spilled. It could have been dangerous, so I had to lecture him about lab safety. He got defensive. Things got a little ugly. But I wasn't fussing at him out of spite. I was lecturing him because safety is very important in the environment where I work."

"And you assume that people will think you killed him because of that?" Hunter clarified, trying to put together the pieces.

Jeremiah's nostrils flared as if he were mentally reliving the moment. "Raef wasn't happy about being corrected. He thought I'd purposefully embarrassed him in front of his new coworkers, and he confronted me after work. We had a pretty heated exchange."

"All because he slipped and knocked over the beaker?" Hunter narrowed his eyes as he listened.

Jeremiah nodded. "Because I called him out on it. He said I had it in for him, and I hadn't liked him from the start, which was ridiculous because I'd never talked to him before that day."

Hunter didn't know Raef very well, but a better picture of the man formed in his mind.

Suddenly, it didn't really surprise Hunter that Abby hadn't been interested. Raef sounded like a piece of work. For a moment, he did wonder exactly who Abby's type was.

It didn't matter, however. That wasn't important to this assignment.

"Why are you telling me this?" Abby leaned toward Jeremiah, curiosity in her gaze.

"I'm sure he told you his side of the story. Made me out to be the bad guy." He scowled again.

"What makes you so sure he told me anything?" She tilted her head as she waited for his response.

"Because the two of you were an item." Jeremiah shrugged as if her question came out of left field.

Abby froze before letting out a nervous—and slightly loud—laugh. "Why in the world would you think that?"

"Because that's what Raef told people around the office."

Her eyes narrowed with confusion. "He did? Are you sure?"

"He was *always* talking about you. About how wonderful you were. About how you were having dinner this week and how excited he was to spend more time with you. He had it bad for you. I mean *bad* bad." Jeremiah rolled his eyes as if he'd thought the whole thing was over the top.

"We only went on one date," Abby corrected. "And that date was the day before yesterday."

Jeremiah shrugged as if he wasn't really listening. "That's not the way Raef made it sound. He indicated that the two of you would probably be married before the end of the summer. He was hoping you might even get married in the theater."

Abby's skin turned paler. "Is that right?"

Jeremiah stepped away from the table as their food was delivered. "Anyway, I'm sorry to interrupt your lunch. But I just wanted to assure you I had nothing to do with his death."

With that statement, Jeremiah turned and stormed out of the restaurant.

But Hunter didn't like the picture that formed in his mind.

So who *was* behind Raef's death? And the even bigger question: why?

At first, he thought this person might be targeting Abby now because she might somehow be able to identify him.

But now it seemed more extreme and nuanced than that.

Especially after he and Axel had nearly been run off the road this morning.

Cadence paused by their table, a frown on her face. "You guys . . . I just found this envelope with Abby's name on it."

She held up a clean business-sized envelope with "Abby" neatly written across the front.

"Where did you find that?" Hunter asked.

"It was left on a table near the bathroom in the back. I looked around—no one was back there."

Hunter used a napkin to take the envelope from her and carefully opened it.

Tension thrummed through the air as he did.

He then pulled out a piece of paper. The words written there were clear, "This isn't how it was meant to be."

He stared at the message before showing it to Abby. "What does this mean?"

Her eyes widened. "I don't know."

His jaw tightened. This guy was still close. Was still watching.

He glanced at Abby and saw the distress written all over her features.

Then he checked the time. "When does this next house have to be cleaned by?"

She blinked several times in surprise, almost as if she'd been lost in another world. "What?"

"When are the new renters checking into the house you're cleaning next?" he repeated.

"Not until the morning. Why?" She narrowed her eyes with curiosity.

"Because I say we finish up lunch here. We drop this off with Cassidy. You figure out your meeting for tonight so you can get that off your mind. Then I think you need to unwind and decompress."

"I would *love* to unwind. But I don't even know how or where to go." Her voice indicated she had no hope that would actually be a reality.

"I have an idea," Hunter said. "Do you trust me?"

"Trust you?" Abby stared at him a moment before nodding. "I do."

He grinned. "Good. So let's eat, get that meeting set up, and then I have the perfect idea to get your mind off things for a while."

———

Abby scaled down the backside of the wall at the obstacle course set up for training at the Blackout campus.

This hadn't exactly been what she had in mind when Hunter had mentioned decompressing.

She'd already crawled through a tunnel, crab walked beneath razor wire—Hunter assured her it wasn't actually sharp, darted through tires placed flat on the ground, and climbed sideways across some type of rope strung between the trees.

She reached the bottom of the traverse wall, where Hunter waited for her, and he let out a cheer. "Good job, Abby."

Abby scowled at him before grabbing the water bottle he held out and taking a long sip.

Then she sat on the edge of the platform to catch her breath. "When you said you wanted me to unwind and decompress, I didn't think it would include cruel and unusual punishment."

"Really?" He sounded truly surprised.

She gave him a look. "Are you *sure* this is a stress reliever?"

"Absolutely. It works for all the guys here, at least."

Thankfully, Hunter had talked her through every one of the obstacles and cheered her on. He'd been an excellent coach. Once, she'd started to fall from the rope walk, and he'd caught her.

She'd been reminded just how solid his muscles were and how steady he was on his feet.

She hadn't complained. She may have even tried to think of other ways she could accidentally fall into his arms. But Abby hadn't taken things that far.

He might catch on to her tactics and think she was flirting with him again.

Hunter was off-limits. She couldn't fall back into her old habits, no matter how tempting it was. She had to be stronger than that, to prove to herself that she wasn't her mother.

She cleared her throat and said, "I'm going to be so sore tomorrow."

"The good news is that you did it." Hunter lowered himself onto the platform beside her.

Abby took another long sip of water. She almost didn't want to admit it, but she did feel good to have accomplished what she might have earlier deemed impossible.

"I did it. You're right—that is good."

She glanced around the Blackout campus where the obstacle course was located. The property was on a stretch of land beside the Pamlico Sound, and it was absolutely gorgeous.

Her mood lightened considerably.

"I've never been here before," she murmured.

"Not many people are allowed inside these gates."

Abby placed a hand over her heart. "I'm so honored."

Even though she might have sounded slightly sarcastic, she meant the words. The fact that Hunter brought her here made her feel special. And being here had distracted her, which was just what she needed.

Her problems still existed. They still lingered just out of sight, ready to pounce when she was least expecting it.

But she'd forgotten about them for a brief moment.

She suddenly didn't want this downtime to be over.

"Let's play Ask Me Anything," she blurted.

He raised his eyebrows.

Abby tried not to stare. But he looked good—really good—even with the sweat spread over his face and dampening his gray T-shirt. Everything about him was so . . . so masculine and alluring. She usually went for the more artsy and desk-job type of guy.

Hunter was nothing like that . . . and she could appreciate the change.

"Ask Me Anything? Really?"

"Really. I'll play nice, I promise."

He took another sip of his water, the sun glinting in his eyes and making them almost look amber. "Okay. What's the penalty for skipping a question?"

"If I skip a question, I'll do the obstacle course again."

He raised his eyebrows. "And what will I have to do?"

She nibbled on her bottom lip a moment. "If you skip, you have to sing a song from my favorite musical right here on this platform for all the world —or, at least, anyone who's around—to hear."

He chuckled. "Fine. But you'll be suffering more than I will. You go first."

"I get the first question?" She raised her eyebrows this time.

"Why not? This was your idea."

She let out a sigh as she thought about what she wanted to ask. "Where are you from?"

"Missouri." He paused. "My turn. Where are you from?"

"Florida." She thought for a moment about her next question. "Are you an only child?"

"No. Are *you*?"

"Yes, as a matter of fact, I am. My mom was a single parent, and she struggled—a lot. She passed away several years ago, but not without leaving a legacy of chaos."

"I'm sorry to hear that."

Abby shifted, wanting to take the attention off herself. "How about you?"

"I have two brothers, and we try to get together as often as possible." He shifted against the sunlight. "Have you always wanted to be an actress?"

"Since high school. My mom always thought that the bug would pass, but it never did." She paused. "How about you with the military?"

"My dad was military, so it only seemed natural. Things like that kind of run in families sometimes." He paused in thought. "Have you ever been married?"

"No. You?"

As soon as Abby asked the question, something darkened in Hunter's gaze.

Something told her he might just be singing that song.

EIGHTEEN

HUNTER SHOULD HAVE REALIZED that Abby would return the question after he asked it. But he wasn't prepared to talk about Stephanie.

He also wasn't prepared to sing a song in front of anyone who might wander past. So he answered.

"Yes." His voice sounded gravellier than he'd hoped. "I was married. But she died."

"I'm sorry. I shouldn't have asked—" Abby's cheeks flushed as the words rushed from her lips.

"Don't be ridiculous." He rose to his feet and stretched before offering his hand to her to help her stand. "But . . . as fun as that was, I'm thinking we should probably get back to work now. What do you think?"

Her soft hand filled his as he pulled her to her feet. "Probably a good idea."

He tugged her up more quickly that he'd intended, and she nearly collided into him. He caught her arms, but they stood close.

Too close.

As in, right against each other.

Abby looked up in surprise, and their eyes met.

Something passed between them, and his gaze went to her lips.

Her full lips. Lips that he would love to kiss. That he'd love to discover how soft they were. How they tasted . . .

Hunter's cell phone beeped and jerked them from the moment.

He took a step back, grateful for the distraction, yet disappointed at the same time. When he glanced at his phone screen, he saw it was Axel.

He quickly answered just in case it was important. It was Axel inviting him to dinner tonight—and Axel insisted he bring someone with him.

Hunter knew exactly who he was talking about. Abby.

He promised to think about it.

As Hunter ended the call, he glanced at Abby. He could read her well enough to know she was only pretending not to pay attention. No doubt she'd heard most of that conversation.

"That was Axel . . ." he started.

Abby smiled. "I've met him before. He seems like a character."

"He is. He invited us to dinner tonight."

"Us?"

He shrugged. "That was what he hinted at . . . but it's just casual. Nothing formal or romantic involved."

"I'm surprised he wants me there."

Hunter shrugged again. "Who knows what he's thinking? Olivia probably gets bored with all our talk about work and wants another woman there. Either way, don't feel obligated. I don't want things to be weird."

Abby shrugged this time. "I think it sounds fun."

Surprise flooded his gaze. "Really?"

"Sure. Why not? I mean, I have to eat."

Hunter nodded slowly. "Great. I'll let him know. Now, before we get back to work, there's something I'd like to show you."

"What is it?" Surprise washed across her features.

"It's here at the Blackout campus." He almost reached his hand out to take hers as they walked.

But he didn't.

Hunter had been hired to protect Abby, even though he wasn't really sure this was actually a paying gig. The fact of the matter was that he didn't care about the money.

He led her across the campus toward the Daniel Oliver Building. The large, three-story structure had opened two years ago, named in honor of one of their fallen comrades.

He paused in front of an old silver Honda Civic. "This is yours."

Abby glanced at the car and then back at him. "What do you mean?"

"You need a car, and I just happened to know a guy getting rid of one. I arranged it so you can have this one."

She stared at him another moment.

Hunter couldn't read the emotion in Abby's eyes. He had no idea what she was thinking, but she clearly didn't look thrilled.

He'd overstepped, hadn't he?

When her mouth opened, he prepared himself to get an earful.

———

Abby stared at the car, her mouth opening and then closing again.

Then she looked back at Hunter.

Her first impulse was that she didn't want anyone's charity.

But she knew by looking at him that he was only trying to help.

Just yesterday, she might have been offended.

But right now, she only felt touched by his thoughtfulness.

Instead of any words leaving her lips, tears filled her eyes.

"I overstepped, didn't I?" Guilt washed over Hunter's features. "I should've asked . . ."

That was when Abby realized he'd totally misread her.

"No, it's not that at all," she insisted. "It's just that . . . I don't remember the last time that anyone did anything so sweet for me. Unless you count the fact that my friends hired you to protect me." She let out a self-conscious laugh.

"So . . . you're not mad?" He studied her face.

"Mad?" Abby stared at him. "Why would I be mad?"

Hunter shrugged. "Some people don't like help. They're offended by it. I didn't think you would be, but I wasn't really sure."

"This is so sweet of you, Hunter." The next instant, she threw her arms around his neck and hugged him tight.

He stood still, almost as if in shock, before finally

wrapping his arms around her and pulling her close also.

The smell of his cologne wafted up to her. He held on a moment longer than Abby had thought he would. But she wasn't complaining.

She'd dreamed about what Hunter's arms might feel like around her.

Now she knew.

Suddenly, he stiffened.

Now *Abby* was the one who'd overstepped.

She quickly pulled back and straightened her clothing, trying not to show just how self-conscious she felt at his rejection.

She needed to use her acting skills to conceal her true feelings right now.

Hunter glanced back at the car, seeming to try to erase the memory of what had just happened also. "I have a few more things I want to check out before handing the keys over to you. I'm hoping I can get around to doing that tonight."

Abby shrugged a little too quickly to play off her embarrassment. "Whatever works for you. I'm just so grateful you did this. Thank you again."

"Of course." He straightened. "We should probably get going, though. How about we do a test drive later?"

Abby grinned, pretending like nothing had just

happened between them and that the awkwardness she'd felt was only imagined. "That sounds great."

But inwardly, she wanted to erase her feelings. To erase the fact that Hunter had probably seen the longing in her eyes. And to erase the slight ache that had formed in her heart.

She couldn't let another man hurt her. She'd too easily begun to let her walls down.

She feared allowing that to continue would only prove to be a mistake.

CHAPTER
NINETEEN

HUNTER COULDN'T FORGET the feel of Abby's arms around him.

He'd been trying to deny his attraction to her ever since he took this assignment.

But as soon as he'd felt her press against him and smelled her flowery perfume, all his resolve was forgotten.

Until he remembered it.

The realization that he shouldn't be hugging her had hit him with a jolt.

He hadn't meant to make Abby feel self-conscious, even though he had a feeling that was exactly what he'd done. She'd covered her feelings pretty well, but he'd seen a flash of hurt in her eyes.

He'd have to be more careful in the future.

He'd never expected to feel this way about

someone else again. The emotions felt foreign . . . or inappropriate. He couldn't pinpoint it exactly.

He only knew the whole situation left him feeling uneasy.

They climbed into his truck and started toward Abby's final job of the day. As he left the complex, he waved to several colleagues who trained outside. The guard at the station opened the gate to let them out.

As they drove over the bridge, Hunter spotted someone pulling a kayak from the small canal beneath it.

He hit his brakes. He was always cautious when he saw anyone in the water near the Blackout campus. The people working there had a lot of enemies from their time in Special Forces. After a few incidents had occurred there, everyone remained vigilant when they saw anyone suspicious around the property.

"Is that . . . ?" Abby stared at the man.

"Do you recognize him?"

"I think that's . . . Peter. Raef's roommate."

Hunter's thoughts raced. Was it a coincidence this guy was here?

He didn't think so.

Because if that guy was pulling his kayak out of the water now, that meant he would have had time to paddle out to the Pamlico Sound, that he could have seen Abby on the obstacle course.

Before the guy could get away, Hunter pulled to the side of the road and threw his truck into Park. Then he climbed out and strode toward the man.

Abby followed on his heels.

"What are you doing?" Hunter demanded as they drew near.

Peter froze, his eyes widened as he looked at Hunter then Abby. "I was fishing."

"Why here? There are plenty of other places on the island."

"I heard this place has the best redfish."

Hunter's gaze went to the black case in his kayak. It was the perfect size for . . . a gun.

"What's in there?" he demanded.

Peter raised his arms. "Just my fish. I promise."

"Open it," Hunter growled. "Slowly."

"Okay, man . . . but I don't know who you think you are. There's nothing here saying I can't launch a kayak." He leaned toward the box and cautiously opened it.

When he did, Hunter peered inside and frowned.

Indeed, it was only a few fish. The black case was a glorified cooler.

"Are you happy now?" Peter glared at him, not bothering to hide his annoyance.

Hunter scowled. "I wouldn't launch here anymore if I were you."

"Why not?"

"We take security very seriously around here. That's all you need to know."

With that, Hunter took Abby's arm and led her back to the truck.

He couldn't take any chances—not considering everything that had happened.

———

As they pulled up to the next house Abby was scheduled to clean, she couldn't stop thinking about seeing Peter in that kayak, so close to where they were on Blackout grounds.

Was that a coincidence? She had a hard time believing it was.

Could Peter really be behind these crimes?

She'd only met the guy once, but she found the idea hard to believe. If Peter had killed Raef, it would have been in the heat of an argument. Abby didn't see any reason why he'd keep coming after her. Besides, the guy didn't even seem to recognize her right now.

Still, Abby needed to be extremely careful who she trusted.

Finally, she and Hunter pulled up to a small, stilted cottage not far from her own place.

It shouldn't take terribly long to get this place clean, but she was grateful Hunter was with her.

Later, she'd still need to go home and get cleaned up before the meeting tonight—especially now that she'd done the obstacle course. She was dirtier and sweatier than she'd like to admit.

She didn't miss the tension stretching between her and Hunter as they rode down the road.

She'd enjoyed their downtime so much that she'd almost forgotten they had a professional wall between them. Despite her inner protests, something had begun to stir inside her.

Something she didn't dare put a name to.

That would make it too real. Too easy to get hurt again.

Hunter had felt something between them too, hadn't he? It wasn't just her.

Either that or Abby was totally misreading the man.

Her head pounded. She didn't know what to think.

Hunter wasn't her type . . . yet the man had surprised her. Maybe she'd been wrong about him. Maybe he wasn't controlling . . . in fact, he only seemed to be looking out for her.

After offering Hunter a tight smile, she opened her door and stepped out. She grabbed the cleaning supplies from the back of his truck and started toward the house. Then she punched in the code and opened the door.

Just as before, Hunter instructed her to stay where she was so he could check out the rest of the place.

She nodded, knowing better than to argue.

He skirted around the inside of the house, checking the living room and kitchen first before heading toward the bedrooms.

As Abby waited, she took several deep breaths.

Everything would be okay.

She had to stop thinking the worst. Had to stop thinking danger was around every corner.

Yet that truly seemed to be the case.

At that thought, she heard a yell, followed by a crash.

She sucked in a breath as panic raced through her.

Had someone been waiting inside the house for them to arrive?

A MASKED MAN had burst out of the closet as Hunter was checking out an open sliding door in one of the bedrooms.

The guy had taken Hunter by surprise and tackled him.

Hunter managed to throw the guy off. But as he turned back toward the intruder, Hunter spotted the Taser in the man's hand.

It was him again. The same guy.

He had to act quickly before he got zapped again.

Because then . . . the guy could go after Abby. Hunter couldn't let that happen.

"Abby . . . run!" he yelled.

He needed to get her out of here. Now.

The man growled and lifted his arm.

As he did, Hunter kicked the man's hand. The

Taser engaged, but the probes missed Hunter.

The device fell out of the man's hand and clattered onto the wood floor.

The man seemed to realize he was now vulnerable.

He raised his fists, ready to fight.

But Hunter got the first punch in.

His fist connected with the man's jaw, and the guy reeled backward.

Before the intruder could catch his breath, Hunter lunged at him again.

If he could just get that mask off . . .

But the man ducked, and Hunter's fist hit the wall instead.

Pain throbbed through his hand.

Hunter grunted as he turned back toward the killer.

The man charged him again.

This time, they spun around, and Hunter fell through the open door and out onto the deck.

Momentum kept him moving.

The next instant, he crashed against the railing of the deck.

Wood splintered.

The railing broke.

And Hunter felt himself falling with his attacker trailing not far behind.

Just as Abby reached the street as she ran away, she heard another crash.

She turned in time to see someone fall from the second-story deck.

No, not someone. *Two* someones.

Her breath caught.

One of them was Hunter.

She looked at the road and remembered Hunter yelling for her to run.

Yet how could she flee when he was in trouble?

She'd already called for backup. The police should be on their way.

But how long would it take them to get here?

She froze and watched as one of the men rose to his feet. Not Hunter.

The other guy.

Abby stared at him as the guy turned toward her. The mask on his face didn't allow her to see who he was.

Yet she was certain the man was looking at her. Contemplating if he should run toward her next.

She could hardly breathe as she waited.

If she started running now, maybe she could get away from him.

Maybe.

But then what would happen to Hunter?

Sirens wailed in the distance.

"Who are you? What do you want?" Abby yelled, trying to distract him. Trying to gain some knowledge of who he might be.

But he didn't speak.

Not that she'd expected him to reveal his identity. She'd yet to hear the man's voice. Was he trying to hide it? Did she know the guy?

The thought caused a chill to race through her.

With one last glance at her, the man darted toward the beach.

Abby released the breath she'd been holding.

Then she snapped into action and ran toward the dune where Hunter had landed.

She had to know if he was okay.

Worst-case scenarios rushed through her head.

She ran under the house and then scrambled up the dune toward Hunter.

But when she found him, his eyes were closed.

He wasn't moving.

Was he . . . dead?

Moisture rushed to her eyes as panic consumed her.

No . . . not Hunter.

Lord, please, not Hunter. Please.

HUNTER'S ENTIRE BODY ACHED.

He pulled his eyes open and blinked several times as he heard someone calling his name.

Everything was blurry, but he thought he saw someone kneeling over him.

He pressed his eyes closed one more time as he tried to stop everything from spinning.

Then he felt a soft hand running along his face. His neck. His arms.

"Hunter?" someone called.

Finally, he opened his eyes again.

Abby leaned over him, the sunlight directly behind her head making her almost look angelic.

"Oh, Hunter . . ." Her voice sounded thick with emotion. "I thought you were dead."

He remembered the fight. Remembered the guy

pushing him from the room and the deck railing collapsing.

Thank goodness, the sand dune had caught his fall. If he'd landed on concrete or anything else, he might not be this lucky right now.

Abby rested her hand on the side of his face as she stared down at him. "I'm so glad you're okay."

Hunter grunted as he forced himself to sit up. Sirens sounded in the distance, and he glanced around as he remembered the intruder.

Where had the man gone?

"He ran down the beach," Abby said, as if reading his thoughts.

Though he was glad that Abby was safe, he wasn't happy the guy had gotten away . . . again.

How did this killer keep managing to do that?

Hunter looked back at Abby again. "I told you to run."

She shrugged. "I know. But I couldn't leave you."

He wanted to fuss at her. But he couldn't.

Her concern was touching.

In fact, the look in her eyes did something strange to his heart. It made him feel something he hadn't felt in a long time. Something he didn't want to feel.

Before they could talk any longer, police vehicles pulled into the driveway.

Cassidy and two officers rushed their way, resolute expressions on their faces.

———

Thirty minutes later, Abby and Hunter were sitting beneath the stilted house in two plastic Adirondack chairs while officers examined the house for evidence.

Paramedics had already checked out Hunter and said he was okay. But they warned him he might be sore for a few days.

Abby thought for sure he'd have a concussion, but apparently, he showed no signs of it. She was thankful for that and for the soft sand that had broken his fall.

"So neither of you got a good look at this guy?" Cassidy clarified as she stood in front of them.

They both shook their heads.

"Unfortunately, no." Hunter rubbed his jaw. "He was wearing a mask and, from the moment I saw him, it was an all-hands-on-deck fight. I wish I could give you something else. I *can* say he moves like a younger guy. He's probably six foot tall, relatively thin, and muscular. I'm not sure if he trusts his physical prowess because he had the Taser with him. To me that signals that he's not someone used to fighting."

"Interesting observation." Cassidy nodded, a hardened, determined look in her eyes. "We found the Taser, and we'll check for prints."

"Good. Do you think it's the guy who killed Raef since he also used a Taser?"

"We assume," Cassidy said. "I also find it strange that Raef died from being strangled. Strangulation usually indicates a sign of passion—it's usually done by an ex-lover or someone close to the victim."

Abby raised her hand and leaned back. "I'm not an ex-lover just in case you're thinking about pointing a finger at me."

Cassidy flashed a slight smile. "That's not what I meant. It's not usually women who strangle men either. It's more a method that men use, and it's usually in the heat of the moment. It's rare that someone plans to kill someone by strangling them with their hands when there are far easier and more effective ways."

Abby shuddered at her words. She didn't know much about crime other than what she read in books and watched on the news. And she didn't want to know any of this firsthand.

But she didn't like the picture of this guy that formed in her mind.

She also kept in mind the description Hunter had presented of the killer. Did that fit anyone she knew? Any of the suspects they were looking at?

She couldn't be sure. Six feet tall and relatively fit seemed to match many of the people she knew, give or take a couple of inches and pounds.

She let out a sigh.

This seemed like the struggle that never ended.

Abby looked over as Florence pulled up at the house. She'd called her boss about fifteen minutes ago to give an update.

Abby had been dreading this talk. Dreading getting in trouble even though this wasn't really her fault.

Would she be fired? She couldn't lose this job. She had no backup plan.

Florence rushed toward her. "Are you okay?"

Abby nodded. "This guy caught both of us by surprise."

Florence shook her head. "I can only imagine. I've already arranged for the incoming renters to use another house. This one obviously won't be safe, not until the decking is repaired."

"Thanks for understanding," Abby said. "I'm sorry all this happened."

Florence patted her shoulder. "It's not your fault.

I'm just sorry about everything you're going through."

"How did this guy get into the house?" Cassidy paced closer to Florence.

The woman frowned. "Most of our houses utilize keypads to get inside. And we change the codes every week, giving different renters different numbers. The housekeeping staff, as well as maintenance all have their own master codes." Her frown deepened. "Every once in a while, we make a mistake and the code from the previous renter doesn't expire exactly when it's supposed to. I suppose that could've happened, but it's doubtful."

"Do you guys keep a log of who uses each security code and when?"

Florence nodded. "We do. I can look into that and let you know."

"I'd appreciate that. What about cameras?"

"Since these are rentals, we can't have cameras. It would be an invasion of guests' privacy. We could probably get away with keeping them on the front door, but most renters don't want them."

"I understand." Cassidy looked back at Hunter and Abby. "I'm glad the two of you are okay. That could have turned out much differently."

"Yes, it could have." Abby ran her hands across her jeans as anxiety seemed to boil inside her.

She glanced at her watch. Her meeting with the cast and crew was supposed to start in an hour.

It looked like she wasn't going to have time to go home and change. She could take off the smock she had to wear when she cleaned. But still, her clothes were sweaty and dirty from the obstacle course earlier.

This wasn't the way she wanted to go into a meeting.

But how she looked wasn't her biggest concern right now.

The fact that someone had almost killed Hunter was.

CHAPTER
TWENTY-TWO

JUST AS HE'D done at the theater, Hunter stood at the back of the church and studied everyone during the meeting.

As before, Abby had a great stage presence and commanded the attention of everyone listening.

His jaw still hurt, as did his shoulder from his earlier fight. But things could have ended so much worse.

Still, he was irritated with himself that the guy had surprised him and that he hadn't caught a glimpse of the man's identity.

The killer just kept coming back for more and more. And Hunter feared what it was going to take to make this guy stop.

He feared it might be another dead body.

His hands fisted at the thought.

His gaze went back to Abby again.

Because he'd been around her a lot over the past couple of days, he knew she was nervous. There was a slight quiver in her voice and her gaze wasn't quite as steady as usual.

But she was holding up remarkably well given the circumstances. He'd thought Abby was the shallow type, but he'd been wrong. She'd overcome a tough upbringing and had made it on her own. She worked hard, she wasn't afraid to get dirty or to try new things.

The woman had truly surprised him.

Hunter shifted his thoughts as he surveyed everyone at the meeting.

Devin and Bruno sat near the front as they listened.

Hunter still wasn't sure if either of those men were truly suspects. Neither quite fit the physical description of the attacker. But he'd keep an eye on them, just in case.

He also needed to watch for anyone else acting suspicious, but so far he'd seen nothing unusual.

As Abby started to explain that the cast and crew were going to need to put a hold on rehearsals, Bruno jumped to his feet. "I came here just to act in this play. If there's no play, then why should I stick around Lantern Beach?"

"I understand your frustration," Abby started, lowering her voice. "I'm frustrated too. But at this point, my hands are tied."

"Can you even guarantee us that the show will go on?" a woman—Danielle, Hunter thought—asked.

Abby frowned. "I wish I could say that, but at this point I'm still gathering information. I plan on having a contractor come look at the place as soon as possible, and I'm hoping he can tell me how long the repairs will take."

"But otherwise, you just want us to wait?" Devin asked. "Because I'm working another job to make ends meet, but living on this island is so expensive that it's tiresome. Without a play, I don't have a reason to stay."

"If you would just give me a little more time before you make that decision." Abby's voice sounded strained under the pressure of the moment.

At once, everyone seemed to talk among themselves, and she lost control of the situation.

Part of Hunter wanted to step up and help her. But she was a strong woman and if she needed help, she'd ask.

His gaze drifted to the back door as someone else stepped inside.

Peter. Raef's roommate.

What was he doing here?

He wasn't affiliated with this play in any way.

Hunter's back muscles tightened as he waited to see what the man might do.

———

Abby felt the meeting spinning out of control, and panic raced through her.

As she glanced at the back of the room, she spotted Peter step inside.

What was *he* doing here?

When she glanced at Hunter, she saw he was watching the man too.

Hunter would handle him if he had to. She felt confident about that.

Right now, Abby needed to concentrate on this meeting.

She clapped her hands to get everyone's attention, and eventually the crowd quieted. "I appreciate that you guys have stuck with me. I know this is hard. The best I can tell you right now is that I can give you an answer by the end of the week. I beg you all to wait until that time to make any decisions. Because if you want to leave, there's no need of getting the theater fixed. Without you, there is no show."

More murmuring spread before she closed out the meeting.

A few people stayed afterward to ask her questions, and she answered them to the best of her ability.

Eventually, everyone filed out, leaving just her and Hunter.

Immense relief filled her.

She glanced at the back of the room. Even Peter was gone. But questions about his presence still lingered in her mind.

Hunter strode up to her and gazed down at her. "Good job. I know they were a tough audience, but you held yourself together well."

"Thanks." But Abby's mind was really on only one thing right now. "What was Peter doing here? Did you talk to him?"

Hunter nodded. "I did. He said he didn't realize earlier that was you when we confronted him on the kayak. He wanted to stop by and offer his condolences."

"His condolences?" Realization washed through her. "Oh, right. Raef told everyone the two of us were dating."

A flicker of amusement flashed in his gaze. "Apparently."

Abby let out a sigh. "I don't even know what to

say. Maybe I should ask Serena to publish an article stating Raef and I were *not* an item."

"Don't bother explaining." He placed his hand on her back. "You don't have to say anything to anybody. You ready to get out of here?"

His reassurance brought her a surprising measure of comfort. "Absolutely."

As they climbed back into Hunter's truck, he turned to her. "I understand if you want to cancel on dinner tonight. It's been a crazy day."

"Are you kidding? It will be good for me. I could use a distraction right now." She looked down at her clothes. "I'm afraid I'm not very presentable."

"I think you look fine." Hunter glanced at his watch. "But if you'd feel better getting cleaned up, we have thirty minutes. We can swing by your place first. I'll just need five minutes back at my place to shower and change."

"If you would take me to my place, it would be amazing."

"Your wish is my command."

She had to smile at his words. As grumpy as Hunter came across, he really wasn't. He was simply reserved, and Abby felt honored he'd actually let her beyond his walls on a few occasions.

Maybe she'd been wrong about him. Maybe he wasn't anything like Michael or Nelson.

Five minutes later, they arrived at her rental. As Hunter checked the place out, Abby felt a flash of fear as she remembered what had happened earlier.

Dear God, please protect him. Protect everyone around me. Keep them safe. Help Cassidy catch the person behind this. I'm begging You for Your help.

She didn't want to see anyone else harmed—especially not Hunter.

Thankfully, he stepped from the hallway and gave her an affirming nod. "All clear."

Abby released her breath.

A few minutes later, she hopped in the shower and scrubbed the sweat and grime from her skin. Then she dressed in some fresh jeans and a white tank top. She slipped on some boots, pulled her still damp hair back into a twist, and put on a touch of makeup.

She felt 100 percent better.

She just needed to decide on what to wear over her tank top.

She leaned out the bedroom door, holding two choices in her hands. "Which one do you think?"

Hunter peered around the corner. He glanced at the burgundy sweater then at the pale yellow one. "The burgundy."

"I thought so too."

A few minutes later, she stepped into the living room.

Hunter's eyes widened with appreciation when he saw her. "You clean up nicely. That sweater is a great color on you."

Abby gave him a little curtsy. "Thank you."

She paused in front of him, and their gazes caught. As they did, she felt something pass between them.

Her heart pounded harder as she was suddenly all too aware of his presence. Of his masculinity. Of how fond she'd grown of him over the past couple of days.

She'd been wrong about him. She felt certain of the fact.

Did he share her feelings?

Abby wanted to say yes, but she just wasn't sure.

But what about the invisible force that seemed to draw them together? That couldn't be her imagination, could it?

You need someone who doesn't tell you what to do. Someone who's more passive. Who won't try to control you. Hunter's not that guy.

An internal voice reminded her of her past mistakes. Yet another part of her thought that internal voice was wrong.

What if Hunter was nothing like she'd assumed?

She nibbled on her lips, unsure.

After a moment of silence, Hunter held his keys in the air.

"We should go." His voice sounded scratchy as he said the words.

Abby pulled herself together and nodded. "Yes, we should."

The sooner she could get herself away from the temptation that was Hunter Bancroft, the better.

CHAPTER
TWENTY-THREE

HUNTER, Abby, Axel, and Olivia had gathered in one of the private dining areas in the Daniel Oliver Building. The place had apartments, where most of the Blackout guys lived. There was also a dining hall, a large-but-cozy lobby, workout rooms, and offices.

Nothing about it felt institutional. Ty Chambers and Colton Locke, who ran the place, had done their best to make it feel homey.

They'd succeeded.

"Hunter will never tell you this." Axel clamped his hand down on his friend's shoulder as they all sat around the table. "But he makes the best chocolate chip cookies ever."

Hunter rolled his eyes. Of course, his friend had brought up that subject. "Those cookies were the biggest mistake I ever made."

Abby grinned as she turned toward him, curiosity in her gaze. "Why is that?"

"Because now no one will forget it, and they keep asking me to make cookies because mine were *soooo* good. I don't even like baking."

A round of laughter went around the room.

It had been a nice night, Hunter realized as he leaned back in his wooden chair.

Axel and Olivia had made creamy Italian sausage pasta for them, along with salad, breadsticks, and chocolate cake for dessert. Based on the way the newly engaged couple giggled, they'd had a great time cooking together.

A moment of envy spread through him. That was how things were supposed to be between him and Stephanie. But their relationship hadn't worked out that way.

The conversation this evening had been easy and had made Hunter realize how much he had missed get-togethers like this.

Ever since Stephanie died, his whole life had revolved around his work. Working seemed easier than remembering the heartache . . . but maybe that was a mistake.

He turned to Abby as he felt the evening winding down. "I should probably be getting you back."

"I guess we should go." Abby offered a gentle

smile. "But this has been a lovely evening. Thank you for including me."

"Anytime," Axel said.

She'd fit right in and had been a great conversationalist. She'd seemed comfortable and at ease with his friends, and the warmth inside her seemed so genuine.

"And congratulations on your engagement," Abby continued. "I can tell the two of you will be very happy together."

Axel and Olivia both beamed.

"Can we help you clean up?" Hunter offered, glancing at the plates on the table.

Axel waved him off. "We've got it. But thank you."

As they wandered from the private dining room, Hunter paused and turned toward Abby. "Would you like to go sit outside for a few minutes before we go?"

Hunter wasn't sure where the question came from. But the idea seemed like a good one—at the moment, at least.

Yet he knew he was treading into dangerous territory.

But he couldn't deny his attraction to Abby any longer. His feelings were becoming more and more clear to him. In fact, he marveled at how their personalities complemented each other and balanced each other out. He felt like a better person when he was with her.

Still, he needed to remain cautious. He couldn't make the same mistakes again. His heart might not survive if he did.

He led her through the lobby—calling hello to Brandon Hale and Finley Cooper as they passed. The two were set to get married in a few weeks, and their wedding had caused a lot of chatter on the campus.

Reaching an exit, Hunter guided Abby outside to a little alcove where some patio furniture had been set up overlooking the water. They sat beside each other on the couch there.

"This is really beautiful," Abby murmured as she gazed at the water.

"It's one of my favorite places to come and think."

"I can see why. It feels so safe. I don't know if it's the large fence around the property or the fact that there are former special forces working here. Probably both."

Hunter grinned. "I was hoping you might feel safe here and could let down your guard some after everything that's been going on."

"It was a really fun night. Thanks for letting me come along."

"Letting you come along? I think I'm the one that

got invited to tagalong here. Axel and Olivia clearly wanted to get to know you better."

Abby let out a laugh.

Hunter reached over and rubbed his shoulder, which was still sore from his earlier fall. He was trying not to show how much his body ached, but it did.

"Your shoulder hurt?" Abby asked.

"It does. But I'll be okay."

"Let me see if I can work some of the tension out. Believe it or not, one of the many jobs I had while I was trying to make it as an actress was as a licensed massage therapist."

"You actually had your license, huh?"

"I thought it might be a nice side hustle, but it was a little too weird for me. It shouldn't be, don't get me wrong. It's an honest profession. But I wasn't comfortable touching just anyone. Different strokes for different folks—literally, I suppose."

"You don't have to . . ." Hunter started to protest.

She rose onto her knees and turned to face him. "But I want to. Do you trust me?"

"I do."

"Then turn that way."

He did as he was asked.

Her hands were like magic as they attacked the

knots in his back. He tried not to let himself relax too much. But that was nearly impossible.

"You're really good at this," he murmured.

"I'm glad it's helping. I *am* a trained professional, after all." She let out a soft laugh.

A moment of silence passed, the only sound that of the slight breeze racing over the water and the limbs from shrubby trees swaying and marsh grasses brushing against each other.

"When we played Ask Me Anything earlier, I told you I'd been married before."

"You did."

"I was actually married for nine years."

Her hands slowed slightly. "Is that right?"

Hunter felt a somberness filling him, and part of him wanted to stop talking. But another part of him really wanted to share with Abby more about his past.

"Her name was Stephanie, and we met at a party a mutual friend threw."

"What happened?" Abby asked quietly.

"She died three years ago."

"Oh, Hunter. I'm so sorry."

He nodded somberly. "She was in a car wreck. Police said her death came quickly. I found a lot of comfort that she didn't suffer."

"It had to be so shocking."

"I've been grieving over her for a long time. Or maybe I've been trying not to grieve. I've stayed busy to avoid thinking about what happened. But it's been a process. I haven't dated at all."

Abby stopped rubbing his shoulders and brushed her hand across his back. The next moment, she leaned forward and pressed her cheek against his as she wrapped her arms over his shoulders. "I'm so sorry, Hunter. I can't imagine what that must have been like."

"Honestly, our marriage was turbulent. She got pregnant and that's why we got married."

"You have a child?" Surprise filled her voice.

"She lost the baby when she was six months pregnant. Stephanie never got over it."

"I'm sorry."

"We probably shouldn't have gotten married. But I thought I was doing the right thing. Still, the two of us weren't compatible."

Abby didn't say anything, only listened.

"I vowed if I dated again, it would only be someone who was boring and responsible—someone who was pretty much just like me."

"That's funny—because I vowed I'd only date someone laid-back and not bossy."

They exchanged a laugh.

"Maybe I was wrong, though. Maybe it wasn't a

personality thing as much as it was a character thing."

"Yeah," Abby said softly. "I get that."

Hunter remained quiet a moment, simply enjoying the feel of Abby's arms around him. Inhaling the scent of her flowery perfume. All too aware of just how close she was.

At once, he shifted to face Abby. Their faces were mere inches apart, and he could see all the gold flecks in her eyes. He could feel her breathing grow shallower.

His gaze shifted from her eyes to her lips. Her full, luscious lips.

Before he could stop himself, he dipped his head toward her. Their lips met. Softly at first. But then growing in intensity as the kiss deepened.

When they finally pulled away, their faces still lingered dangerously close to each other's.

"I shouldn't have done that," he whispered. "You're my client."

"But I never hired you."

"But you're still my client."

"Fine." Abby ran her finger along his jaw. "You're fired."

Hunter let out a laugh.

Then he went in for another kiss.

Abby couldn't stop thinking about that kiss.

Correction: those *kisses*.

Because she felt like she could stay out here forever wrapped in Hunter's embrace.

She didn't want this evening to end, even though she knew it had to.

She settled back against him, and he wrapped his arms around her. They quietly stared at the water together, a moment of peaceful bliss falling over them. For just a moment longer, Abby would remain in his arms and pretend like her problems didn't exist.

She ran her fingers along his, relishing the feel of his skin against hers.

"I thought you hated me," she finally admitted.

His biceps twitched. "Hated you? Why would you think I hated you?"

"Because when I tried to flirt with you, it was always a total disaster. Then there was the town social beneath the pier . . ."

People had been dancing to some live music, eating food provided by local restaurants, and generally having a good time. Abby had tried to strike up a conversation with Hunter about ice cream, of all things—probably because she'd just been talking to Serena about her ice cream truck, Elsa.

Hunter had only stared at her as if she'd escaped from a carnival sideshow.

"You tried to flirt with me?" he murmured in her ear.

"Oh, come on. You're not that naive. You had to have noticed." Abby glanced back at him and saw the smile slide across his face. She playfully slapped his arm. "You did notice!"

He shrugged nonchalantly. "Maybe I did. But I didn't come here looking for romance, so I didn't want to lead you on."

"I get that." She understood where he was coming from.

"What about you? You never really said anything about your love life. But certainly, you've dated before."

Abby's smile slipped just slightly. "I have. I've really only had a few serious relationships. My last two were complete disasters. Both guys were charming and handsome on the outside, but full of chaos on the inside. That's part of the reason I decided to leave both Florida and Myrtle Beach."

"Oh, yeah? You ever talk to either of those guys anymore?"

Abby shook her head. "No, Nelson actually

died. But, in truth, I pretty much dated them one right after the other and didn't give myself time to heal in between. After that, I was over men. They just ended up causing me too much emotional turmoil."

"I'm sorry to hear that. But I guess we all go through some bad relationships before we find a good one."

"Which is why when I met you," she leaned toward him and planted another quick kiss on his lips, "I flirted."

"And I was a beast." He grinned.

Abby shrugged. Not so long ago, she hadn't imagined Hunter had such a sweet, tender side.

But he did. A wonderfully sweet and tender side.

Despite the awful week she'd had, right now all that was forgotten.

Until her phone rang.

She hesitated before glancing at the screen.

It was Danielle.

Abby frowned.

Had there been more fallout after their meeting? Was Danielle calling to quit?

Abby stiffened as she stared at the phone and contemplated whether to answer.

She might as well satisfy her curiosity and get this over with.

"I need to take this," Abby said before placing the phone to her ear. "Hello?"

"Abby, you'll never believe this." Danielle's breathless voice sounded over the line.

"Believe what?" But Abby already didn't like where this conversation was going.

"I was leaving the church with CJ. The two of us decided to go to the beach for a few minutes. When we got there, this man wearing a ski mask appeared out of nowhere and attacked CJ."

Abby's breath caught. "What? Is he okay?"

Hunter's muscles bristled beneath Abby's fingers.

"I was afraid the man would kill him. This guy started beating CJ. Then this group of teens appeared farther down the beach. They were being loud and rambunctious. I think they scared the guy away."

Abby's heart pounded harder as she pictured it all happening. "Oh, Danielle. Are you both okay?"

"We are now. We called the police, and they took our statements. But I wanted to let you know. I mean, first Raef died and now CJ was attacked. Is someone trying to knock off members of the cast and crew? Because, if that's the case, I'm out."

"I'm glad you called, but let's give this a little more time before anyone makes any rash decisions, okay? Tell CJ I'm praying for him."

Suddenly, memories of Abby's fun evening were forgotten.

She gave Hunter the update.

Abby knew by his stormy expression that he wasn't happy with the news either.

Someone else had been hurt.

When would the madness end?

CHAPTER
TWENTY-FOUR

AS HUNTER HEADED BACK to Mac and Tali's place with Abby, he longed to get his mind off everything that had happened on the island this week.

But he couldn't, especially not with the newest update Abby had just given him.

Why would someone go after CJ? What sense did that make?

It *had* to be the same guy who was behind these other crimes.

When Raef had been murdered, Hunter had assumed it was because of someone at his job or for personal reasons. Then the guy had come after Abby, and he thought maybe she was the intended target. But now that CJ had been attacked, it almost seemed as if someone was targeting people associated with the theater.

Hunter needed to think that through more because the details didn't all make sense to him.

He reached over and grasped Abby's hand as he drove, sensing her angst over everything. She was usually talkative, but she was quiet now—clearly contemplating everything that had happened.

He wished he could take away her pain, but he couldn't.

All he could do was try to keep her safe—and help figure out what was going on here.

How did CJ's attack fit into all of this? Was it a separate crime?

Hunter had a hard time believing that.

But as time went on, things were making less sense instead of more.

Headlights suddenly appeared behind them.

His muscles tensed at the sight of them.

"Hunter?" Abby's voice quivered as she sensed something was wrong.

Where had this driver come from? No one had been on the road behind them a minute ago. Hunter had been checking.

But he'd also allowed himself to be distracted— by the case. By Abby.

He should have known better.

The one thing Hunter knew for sure was that he couldn't fail Abby like he'd failed Stephanie.

He let go of Abby's hand and gripped the wheel with both hands as he braced himself for whatever might happen next.

The car revved its engine before slamming into the back of his truck.

They careened toward the ditch at the side of the road.

"Hold on!" he yelled as he tried to right his vehicle.

It was too late.

His tires caught on the sandy shoulder.

The next instant, they lurched to a stop as his truck collided with the embankment beside him. The airbags deployed, filling the space in front of them and sending a fine powder into the air.

His gaze darted toward Abby, and he saw the dazed look on her face. Concern pulsed through him.

"Are you okay?" he rushed.

She nodded stiffly, almost uncertainly. "I . . . I think so. You?"

Hunter didn't answer. Instead, he twisted his head to look behind him.

The car was still there. Just what was this guy planning next?

He didn't want to know.

"Stay down," Hunter grumbled.

Abby sank low in her seat.

Hunter glanced at the car again.

The driver had stepped out.

Hunter could see his silhouette as the man crept closer.

Hunter grabbed his gun and slipped out, ready to fight for Abby's safety with everything he had inside him.

"I wouldn't come any closer if I were you," he growled as he raised his Sig.

The man paused and stepped back.

Hunter waited with anticipation to see what this guy would do.

He didn't think the man had a gun. That didn't seem to be his MO. But he couldn't be certain. The guy could have another Taser on hand.

The next instant, the guy darted back inside his vehicle. In record time, the killer threw his car into Drive and squealed away.

He was gone.

Abby was safe, Hunter realized.

For now.

But things could have turned out so much differently.

————

Abby wanted desperately to bask in the warm glow she felt after everything that had transpired between her and Hunter tonight.

But she couldn't. Her thoughts kept going back to tonight's accident. To CJ.

Officer Dillinger had shown up to take their report. A tow truck had to be brought in to get Hunter's once-immaculate truck out of the ditch.

She knew he loved that truck and had taken such good care of it.

Now, it would need a lot of work to restore.

Abby knew she shouldn't feel guilty, but she did. He wouldn't have gotten into that accident if it hadn't been for her.

Everyone around her was suffering. She was at the center of all this.

Hunter had stayed with the truck while Officer Dillinger had given her a ride back to the bookstore.

Abby sat on the window seat near her bed now as she reflected on everything that had happened.

As soon as the accident occurred, she'd seen something change in Hunter. He'd practically hardened before her eyes.

The killer had just taken this to the next level, hadn't he?

If Hunter hadn't had his gun with him, Abby shuddered to think of what may have happened,

Then there was CJ . . .

Why had someone attacked him? Did this have anything to do with the other incidents that occurred at the theater? It almost seemed like the crimes had to be connected.

The fact CJ had been attacked only added to her confusion.

Her thoughts wandered back to her mom—a woman Abby had desperately tried not to emulate. Her mom had done her best. But Abby's childhood had been as tumultuous as the ocean during a storm.

More times than Abby could count, she and her mother had packed their things up to move to another place. Sometimes it was because of a man. Sometimes it was because of a job. Sometimes it was just because her mom said that she needed a fresh start.

But Abby had adopted somewhat of a nomad lifestyle.

Her thoughts drifted to the past several years since she'd finished college. She'd gotten her office job, which she'd kept for only a few years. Then she'd gotten her license as a certified massage therapist and had begun doing theater on the side.

During that time, Abby had stayed in Florida. She'd lived there for the longest stretch of time in her entire life: six years. But after things went south with

Nelson, that ended that streak. She'd moved on to Myrtle Beach afterward.

At first, Nelson had seemed like a nice enough guy. He was an engineer with a steady job. But, beneath the surface, he'd had a lot of issues. Most of them stemmed from the fact that his wife had died of an aneurysm when she was only twenty-six—a year before Abby and Nelson had met.

He hadn't truly gotten over his wife's death, and that had ultimately led to their breakup. Only a few months ago, she'd gotten word he died in a fire at his home.

Abby had vowed for the longest time that she'd never date another widower. It had been too hard. She'd seen the comparison in Nelson's eyes every time she did something. And he'd talked about his wife all the time, about what she was like and how wonderful she was.

Abby admired that he held his wife in such high esteem. But it did make for some awkward conversations and the vague feeling that Abby would never live up to his wife's legacy.

Eventually, he'd become controlling. It was like so much of life had been out of his hands that he desperately wanted to be in charge of whatever he could—including Abby.

But Abby was never meant to be controlled. In

fact, nothing got her more riled up than being told what to do.

Their whole relationship had been a disaster.

Unfortunately, her time dating Nelson had tainted her feelings on things, even though she didn't want it to.

Now, here she was falling for another widower. Hunter seemed different, though.

Still, he *did* have that haunted look in his eyes on occasion, especially when his wife was mentioned. He'd said it had been three years since she died.

In some ways, Abby supposed a person never truly got over the death of a spouse. But was three years truly long enough to move on?

Abby wanted to think it was. But so many questions still swirled in her head.

She glanced outside at the ocean as the moonlight glinted off it.

Lantern Beach certainly was a beautiful place. Though she'd lived at other beaches before, somehow this one outshone them all.

As she stared at the rolling waves, movement caught her eye.

She glanced near the dunes and thought she saw a shadow.

When she blinked, it was gone.

Had someone been out there watching her?

She blinked again, studying the landscape for any signs that what she'd seen was real and not her imagination.

But there was nothing.

Maybe Abby was just imagining things.

Despite that, she let the curtain drop, and crept away from the window as ice-cold fear filled her chest.

It was only a matter of time before this guy struck again.

What if next time he succeeded and someone else ended up dead?

The thought caused a cry to lodge in her throat.

AS CASSIDY WALKED toward The Crazy Chefette the next morning, she was pleasantly surprised to run into Jonah Gray and Rachel Atwood just as they were leaving. She'd gotten to know both of them over the past month.

Both were newcomers to the island, except for the fact that Rachel had spent summers growing up here and actually knew Ty. She worked for Ocean Essence.

Meanwhile, Jonah worked for a different private security group. Cassidy had been cautious of the man when they'd first met, but she'd started to warm up to him more.

Both Rachel and Jonah smiled when they saw Cassidy, and they paused outside the door.

"How's it going, guys?" Cassidy glanced at them.

"Can't complain," Jonah smiled as he held

Rachel's hand and turned away from the early morning sunlight. "You?"

"I've been staying busy."

"So I've heard." Rachel tilted her head. "I'd forgotten just how fast word spreads around a small town like this, especially when bad things happen. That man's murder has been the talk of the island."

"I've definitely had my hands full this week. But I'm hopeful we'll catch this guy soon."

"I hope so," Rachel said.

Cassidy shifted as her thoughts turned to a different subject. "Listen, how are things going at Ocean Essence?"

Someone working at the lab had nearly killed Rachel about a month ago. Thankfully, everything had turned out okay in the end. But the situation had been tense, to say the least.

Rachel didn't smile reassuringly as Cassidy had thought she might. "I guess it's going okay."

"Did you know Raef?"

Rachel frowned and shook her head. "Not really. He hadn't worked there that long. But I'm sorry to hear about what happened."

"We all are." Cassidy shifted. "If you don't mind me asking, did he have any enemies there?"

Again, Rachel shook her head. "I don't think so. As you probably know, he and Jeremiah had that argument. But it was really just a work conflict, not anything that I would think would lead to murder."

Cassidy wasn't quite ready to let the subject drop. "You don't think Raef might have . . . I don't know . . . overheard something he shouldn't have while he was at work?"

It was a theory she'd been playing with, one that seemed worth exploring.

She still didn't trust everything happening at that lab.

Rachel frowned. "It's hard to say. I want to believe everything there is on the up-and-up. But I'm cautious, especially since things still don't seem to have calmed much since then."

"What do you mean?" Cassidy narrowed her eyes.

"There's still a lot of whispering, and maybe even some paranoia. Ever since someone tried to steal that formula, everyone at the office has been on guard, probably because they fear something like that might happen again."

"I know they hired Blackout to offer round-the-clock protection outside the building."

Rachel nodded. "I don't know whether that makes me feel better or worse. I mean, it's good to know security measures are in place. But it's chilling to know they're needed."

Cassidy couldn't agree more.

She gave one more glance at Rachel and Jonah before locking gazes with Rachel. "If you hear anything, please let me know."

Rachel nodded. "I will."

Cassidy went inside to grab a bite to eat. She'd heard from Florence last night about the door code. The person who'd last used the code to get into the rental house yesterday before Hunter's attack was a maintenance worker named Thomas Judge. However, Thomas was out of town on vacation this week.

Somehow, someone else had gotten their hands on his code.

Cassidy was trying to contact Thomas but hadn't had any luck yet.

She would make this visit to the restaurant quick. Then she had more people to talk to . . . because this investigation was dragging on for entirely too long.

TWENTY-SIX

THE NEXT MORNING, Abby climbed out of bed early. It was Wednesday, and the bookstore was officially closed today. The book club ladies had decided to come for breakfast, so Abby needed to get ready.

She'd had a restless night, but she was looking forward to talking to her friends.

As she climbed out of bed and stretched, she wandered toward the window to glance out at the beach. Seeing the ocean in the morning always made her feel better, and she could already see the sun shining outside, promising that today would be a better day.

She was scheduled to meet with the reporter about the accident at the theater and to talk about the future of the play. She also had two houses to clean.

At some point, her schedule would need to return

to normal. Maisie would be back from her trip in a few days, and Abby wouldn't have a bedroom to use here at Mac and Tali's place any longer.

Life was going on despite the danger around her.

She needed to adjust to that.

As she glanced at the shore, she squinted.

Something about the sand looked different.

It almost looked like someone had written a message on the beach outside the bookstore.

It probably said "Joe and Amy Forever" or some other message that tourists liked to create and then take pictures of in order to remember their vacation.

The waves were already beginning to wash the words away as high tide came in.

She squinted again.

From her vantage point in her room, she could almost read what it said—much easier than someone who was standing on level ground would be able to.

Did that say . . . ?

Abby's breath caught.

No, she was seeing things that weren't there.

Yet she wasn't.

Someone had written a message in the sand.

A message specifically for Abby.

The words chilled her.

. . .

I've come for you.

The killer had left that, hadn't he?

She knew he had.

A cold sweat spread across her skin.

————

Hunter hadn't slept last night.

He had too much on his mind.

The accident last night had stirred something inside him.

Memories of Stephanie's death. Of the questions surrounding it. Of his inability to find answers.

If he'd only been more alert in the weeks before Stephanie had died, maybe she'd still be here right now. But work had distracted him.

He wouldn't let another diversion draw his gaze from what he should be focused on.

He'd been hired to protect Abby, and he'd never forgive himself if he let his feelings get in the way of doing just that.

He was already on his way to meet her. He needed to let her know she should clear her schedule today. The safest thing she could do at this point was to stay inside.

Hunter knew that wouldn't be what Abby wanted to hear. But every time she went out, she put herself in danger.

Until this guy was caught, hunkering down was really the wisest choice of action.

He knew Abby was supposed to meet with that reporter today at the theater site. He knew she needed to spread the word about the theater since some people—including many from out of town—had already purchased tickets for the upcoming play. She also had more cleaning jobs lined up, but it wasn't safe to go in those houses either.

His carelessness last night could have gotten them killed. He'd been distracted again. That wasn't okay.

He glanced at his watch.

Abby had mentioned having breakfast with her friends at the bookstore this morning. He didn't want to intrude on that.

If he got there while they were eating, he'd wait outside until they were done.

But then they needed to buckle down.

He prayed Abby would handle the news okay.

Hunter didn't want to fight about it, but he would do whatever it took to keep her safe.

TWENTY-SEVEN

ABBY, Cadence, Serena, and Tali stood upstairs in Mac and Tali's apartment and stared at the beach below.

Half of the eerie message was gone, erased by the waves.

But enough of it remained that everyone got the gist.

They couldn't stop staring at the ominous words.

Mac had already called it in to the police, and he'd also sent them a picture that Abby had taken earlier. But there was nothing Cassidy and her crew could do at this point. Clearly, the person who left the message was long gone.

But their threat was loud and clear.

"I like this less and less all the time." Cadence rubbed her arms as she shivered.

"You and me both." Abby turned away from the window, a new somberness washing over her.

She'd had visions of telling her friends all about the kiss she and Hunter had shared last night.

But now all that giddiness was gone.

All she could think about at the moment was CJ. About last night's accident. About the message left in the sand.

Danger was no longer creeping closer.

Danger was running toward her at full force.

The realization made nausea churn inside her.

Just then, Abby's phone buzzed.

She glanced at the screen, expecting to see it was Hunter calling.

Instead, an unknown number appeared.

Someone had sent her a text.

Even though caution tightened her spine, she clicked on it anyway.

Abby blinked at what she saw.

Several pictures of Hunter popped up. Hunter with a woman.

At first, Abby had thought the photos were of her and Hunter. The woman shared the same dark hair, and it was long and straight just like Abby's.

But the woman with Hunter wasn't Abby.

Her breath caught.

Who was she? Did Hunter already have a girlfriend?

Then the words beneath the pictures came into view.

Don't be fooled. You're simply Stephanie's replacement.

Abby's mind swirled as realizations hit her.

That woman in the picture was Stephanie?

The person who'd sent this message had a valid point.

The similarities between the two women were almost eerie.

Almost like it had been with Nelson.

Her thoughts continued to race.

"Abby?" Tali's voice pulled her from her thoughts.

Should Abby show these pictures to her friends? She'd never even told them about Nelson and the ordeal she'd gone through with him.

Suddenly, the similarities seemed too great to ignore.

She held up her phone. "Someone sent pictures of Hunter's deceased wife."

They all leaned closer.

Serena gasped. "Wow . . . she looked a lot like you."

Abby felt halfway numb as she nodded. "She really did, didn't she?"

Cadence's perceptive gaze caught hers. "What are you thinking, Abby?"

She wanted to try to make sense of her thoughts and feelings right now.

But she couldn't.

Because life seemed to be a series of patterns. Of repeating past mistakes.

Was that what she was doing right now with Hunter?

Was she drawn to men who were still grieving their deceased spouses? Who would do anything to have their wives back . . . including trying to find a similar replacement?

Nausea gurgled inside her at the thought.

———

At precisely nine o'clock, Hunter climbed from the vehicle he'd borrowed from Blackout and strode toward Beach Bound Books and Beans.

Mac unlocked the door when he saw Hunter coming and gave him a nod as he stepped inside. "The ladies are upstairs. Why don't you just go up there and knock? I'm trying to fix a leak in the bathroom."

"Sounds good." Hunter climbed the steps, his apprehension growing as he did.

He'd been praying he'd have the right words. That Abby would understand why she needed to take extra precautions.

But the fact of the matter was this conversation might not be pretty. He wasn't sure exactly what to expect.

Hunter knocked at the door at the top of the stairs, and Tali answered a moment later. She had a strange expression on her face, one he didn't know how to read. But she opened the door wider to let him inside.

As soon as he stepped in, he noticed the tension in the air.

Had something else happened?

His gaze met Abby's.

After everything they'd shared last night, he'd hoped that seeing her today would be a sweeter reunion.

But maybe it was a good thing it wasn't. He had to stay focused.

"Abby?" he started.

"How about if we go downstairs, ladies?" Tali pointed toward the door. "Let's give them some privacy."

The women filed out, but not before Serena cast Hunter a dirty look.

A dirty look? What was that about?

Finally, it was just him and Abby.

She didn't say anything so Hunter started.

"I know this isn't what you want to hear, but you need to clear your schedule today."

She blinked. "What?"

"It's not safe for you to leave anymore. Not until we know who this guy is and what he's planning. Every time you go out there, it's a risk."

"I understand that, but I still have jobs to do. I still have that newspaper interview that's been set up for weeks."

"You're going to have to cancel." As soon as Hunter said the words, he knew they'd come out wrong. He could see that by the flare of anger in Abby's eyes.

She raised her chin. "I don't think that's up to you to decide."

"I'm not trying to tell you what to do. But it's my job to keep you safe. In order to do that, you're going to have to listen to me."

More tension stretched across her expression. "If I remember correctly, I fired you last night."

Her words almost felt like a slap in the face.

Because when she'd said those words to him last

night, it had been because of the feelings developing between them.

She only brought this up out of anger.

Why was she so angry? Maybe Hunter was coming on too strong, and he needed to reframe his statement.

"Look . . ." He started to step closer and touch her arm, but she pulled away.

He got *that* message loud and clear.

"I just need . . . I just need some space," she muttered.

He bristled, hearing the undertone in her words. She thought they'd jumped in too quickly also. But her statement somehow felt final.

"What happened?" The question came out hoarse and throaty with emotion.

"Too much. Too much has happened. And apparently, I'm a creature of habit." She squeezed the skin between her eyes as if fighting tears.

What did that even mean? Hunter had no idea.

"Abby . . ." he started, trying desperately to find the right words.

"Look, I'll stay in this apartment. For now. But I just need to be alone and figure some things out."

"Is this about me? Something I did?"

"It's complicated," she muttered. "But right now, I don't know what I want. I don't know if I should stay here and keep beating this dead horse as I try to get the theater off the ground. If I want to keep working cleaning jobs just to barely make rent and buy groceries. Or if I'm falling back into my old habits—in multiple ways, including romantically speaking."

That had been a jab at him, hadn't it?

Hunter wasn't sure where it had come from.

"I don't need your services anymore," she said the words softly and almost with regret.

Part of him wanted to think this was better. He had needed to tell her anyway that the two of them needed to take a step back until these crimes were resolved. He couldn't risk something else happening to her because he was distracted.

But this wasn't the way he had seen everything working out.

He looked at her one more time before stepping back.

Was this it between them? The last time they would speak?

An ache formed in his chest at the thought.

For now, he needed to respect her wishes and get out of here.

However, he was going to have a lot on his mind for the rest of the day.

TWENTY-EIGHT

ABBY HEARD the knock at her bedroom door, followed by Cadence's soft voice asking, "Can I come in?"

"Okay." Abby pulled her knees to her chest as her thoughts continued to churn.

The door opened, and Cadence slipped inside, closing it behind her. Her friend gently sat on the edge of the bed and observed her a moment.

"Everything okay?" Cadence finally asked.

Abby used her sleeve to wipe away the tears flooding from her eyes. She didn't expect to have a strong reaction like this, but she had.

"It's really a long story," she started with a sniffle.

"I have time," Cadence said. "And I've been told I'm a good listener."

"You are. It's just . . ." Abby shook her head.

She really didn't want to get into this, but maybe it would help to talk everything through. She'd tried to bury the memories. Maybe her reaction was too strong.

But maybe it wasn't.

"When I lived in Florida, I dated this guy named Nelson," Abby started. "At first, he marked off everything on my list. He seemed perfect. We'd been dating about a month when he told me he'd been married before."

"Okay . . ."

"After that, things between us started getting weird. Nelson gave me a new perfume. I didn't love it, but I wore it because he liked it. Then he gifted me some new clothes." She did air quotes around "new clothes." "Turns out the clothes weren't really new. They were his deceased wife's."

Cadence's eyes widened. "Wow . . . that is weird. And the perfume?"

"It was the same scent his wife wore."

"Oh my . . ."

"It just kept getting weirder. I finally realized Nelson was dating me because he wanted to replace his wife—like, carbon-copy replace. I was *never* going to be like his ex-wife. The way he started acting made me uncomfortable. That's why I finally moved to Myrtle Beach—just to get away from him. The truth is, as weird as it was, I also felt sorry for him because his grief was so deep."

Cadence shifted and narrowed her eyes. "So you think Hunter is doing the same thing? He doesn't strike me as the type who's off like that."

"You saw that picture of his wife." Her gaze clouded with tears. "The two of us look a lot alike."

"A lot of people have a certain type that they go for."

"He told me that I should wear a burgundy shirt last night. In almost all those photos, his wife was wearing a burgundy shirt."

Cadence frowned. "I still think you're reading too much into this."

"Today he came in and started telling me what to do. It reminded me so much of Nelson when he tried to control my schedule, to control what I wore, what I ate."

"I understand that must have been jarring . . ."

Abby wiped her tears again. "Maybe I just need a moment to catch my breath. I can't go through what I went through in Florida again. I need time to think."

Cadence squeezed her hand. "I understand. You let me know what I can do for you, and I'm there."

Abby nodded, grateful for her friend. "Thank you."

But she wasn't sure there was anything anyone could do to fix this situation.

———

When Hunter left the bookstore, he called his boss, Colton Locke, and told him that his job was off for today.

He didn't give any more details, only said that Abby had refused his services. Thankfully, Colton hadn't asked too many questions.

"Anything else you need me to do?" Hunter asked instead. He needed something to keep himself distracted.

His only comfort was in knowing that Mac had offered to stay home today to keep an eye on Abby.

"As a matter of fact, there is. I was going to send Titus out to do this morning's shift at Ocean Essence, but he needs to have his shoulder checked out after his last assignment. His appointment should only take a few hours. But if you could cover that time, that would solve some of our problems."

"I just need to keep an eye on things outside the building, correct?"

"That's right. Maddox is there now, but he's

waiting for someone to relieve him since the night shift is over."

"I'll head out that way now then." Hunter felt heaviness press on his chest as he said the words.

Maybe it was better this way. He'd gotten wrapped up in a whirlwind he'd never anticipated. He didn't want to repeat the mistakes of the past. That seemed to be the path he was headed down.

Yet Abby wasn't Stephanie. He knew that.

He and Stephanie should have never gotten married. They shouldn't have done a lot of things. Their whole relationship had been a matter of correcting mistakes, which had then only led to more mistakes.

Had one of those mistakes resulted in her death?

That question still haunted him.

He drove south on the island toward the lab. The two-story, state-of-the-art building was brand new and located on a secluded part of the island, surrounded by marsh grass and beautiful waters.

He parked in the lot and then met Maddox. "Everything going okay here?"

Maddox shrugged. "Pretty boring unless you count some monster mosquitoes that came out at dawn and tried to carry me away."

"I thought they weren't out yet."

"They're out early, and they're vicious."

"Noted. I'll be here for the next several hours. Hopefully, the sunlight will make them scarce."

"For your sake, I hope that's the case. Have fun." Maddox gave him a salute before walking to his own vehicle.

Hunter paced the perimeter of the property, trying to remain on guard from any potential threats to the cosmetics lab.

Why would a cosmetic lab have so many threats against it?

Having round-the-clock security seemed like overkill. But what did he know?

Besides, he had other things to worry about.

No matter where he and Abby stood, he still wanted her to be safe. He still wanted to know who had killed Raef. Who was trying to hurt her.

His phone rang. He saw the name on the screen. Jenny Olson.

Stephanie's best friend.

The woman had largely avoided his calls since Stephanie's death.

She'd finally gotten around to calling him back it appeared.

He pressed the phone against his ear. "Hey, Jenny."

"Hunter." Her voice sounded stiff. "You've been trying to reach me?"

"And you haven't been answering."

"Sorry. It's not personal. I've just had a lot going on. What's up?"

"I haven't been able to stop thinking about Stephanie's death. And recently I discovered she took all the money out of our savings account about a month before she died. I'm trying to figure out why and what happened to that money. I was hoping you might have some answers."

"Money?" she stuttered as she repeated it. "I don't know—"

"Jenny, if anybody knows, it would be you. Please, I need to know what happened. Was someone threatening her? Was she in some type of trouble?"

"Threatening her?" She let out a nervous laugh. "No, nobody was threatening her."

"So you *do* know what happened."

Silence stretched for a moment. "It's not what you think."

"Was she getting ready to leave me?" Saying the words aloud caused a jolt to slam through him. He didn't want to think that was the case, but it would explain the missing money.

"Hunter . . ."

"Just tell me."

"I don't want to taint who you think she was."

"What does that mean?" He tried to keep the surprise out of his voice, but he couldn't.

"Hunter . . ." She paused again. "Are you sure you want to know?"

"I'm sure." Then he braced himself for whatever she had to say.

CHAPTER
TWENTY-NINE

ABBY HAD TRIED to call Florence to cancel her cleaning jobs for the day, but her boss hadn't answered. That was unusual, but maybe Florence was caught up in a meeting and couldn't talk right now.

She'd also tried to call the reporter, but she'd had to leave a voicemail. Despite Hunter's approach, she understood where he was coming from. She didn't appreciate his method, however.

The stress of everything was simply dragging her down and making her want to climb back into bed and try to sleep away her problems.

She was stronger than this. She'd pulled herself out of some hard times before—thanks to lots of prayers and the help of good friends.

But sometimes a girl simply needed a day to figure things out.

That was what Abby needed now.

Time to think.

When a soft knock sounded at her door, she straightened, running a hand through her hair so she wouldn't look as pathetic as she was sure she did.

She called, "Come in," and Tali stepped inside.

"Hey, sweetie. I'm surprised you're still here. Do you want to talk?"

Abby shook her head, unsure why Tali was surprised she was still here. "Not really."

"Don't wait too long to talk to Hunter, okay? It's not fair to him. Though I'm not sure about everything that's going on, sometimes these types of issues can be worked out with just a simple conversation."

"I know we need to talk. I just need some time first."

"Sometimes when we have unresolved issues in our past, they become our baggage today. That's why it's so important that we try to resolve things. I can't tell you what to do, and I know you may not appreciate my advice. But talk to him. Don't sit on it too long. You'll regret it if you do."

"You're right. Thank you."

Tali took a step away but paused. "Also, I was

surprised to get the text from you. And I'm surprised you're still here."

Abby blinked. "What text?"

She had no idea what Tali was talking about.

"The one you sent to me, Cadence, and Serena."

"Tali . . . I didn't send a text."

She frowned before pulling out her phone and showing Abby the screen. A text message with Abby's name as sender appeared.

> Can we meet at the theater this morning at eleven? I need to talk. It's urgent.

Abby's heart pounded harder.

She glanced at the time. It was almost eleven now.

"Tali, that wasn't me." Her voice quivered.

Tali drew in a breath. "If not you, then who?"

Abby's thoughts raced.

Someone must have cloned her cell phone.

Had the killer sent that message? But why?

She thought she knew.

Someone had wanted to lure her friends out.

The question was: what did this person want to do with them when he did?

Abby shot out of bed.

She had to warn them.

Now.

———

"One weekend, while you were deployed, a few of us girls went up to Atlantic City for a girls' trip," Jenny said.

"Okay . . ." Hunter kept an eye out for trouble around Ocean Essence as he waited for Jenny to continue.

"She started playing slot machines. It seemed like innocent fun at the time. She loved it. I mean like she really got this kind of emotional high from it. So then she moved on from there to play some of the tables. And she won big that weekend. Ten thousand dollars."

"What?"

"It's true. But unfortunately, she wasted some of it on a celebration meal, some shows, some shopping." Jenny paused. "If I'd known then what we started that weekend, I would've never suggested we go there."

"What exactly started that weekend?" Hunter thought he knew the answer, but he wanted to ask the question anyway.

"She became addicted, Hunter. Stephanie thought that gambling was the answer to her problems."

"Oh no."

"She missed having money. When she got a taste

of what it would be like to have some wealth again, she couldn't get enough of it. I begged her to tell you. And I begged her to stop. But she always said: just one more time."

Hunter shook his head, unable to believe what he was hearing. "I don't know what to say . . ."

"I know it doesn't sound like the Stephanie you knew and loved. But she had a reckless side that came out sometimes. We went to Atlantic City again the weekend before she died. She said she had a feeling she was going to make it big. And so she brought a lot of money with her."

"And?"

"She lost it all. She was devastated. She thought that you were going to leave her once you found out."

"I wouldn't have done that. But . . . I just can't believe this. I had no idea this was going on."

"She was so upset," Jenny continued. "You were due to come home in another week, and she didn't want you to see what she had become."

"So the accident . . . ?" He didn't want to finish the question.

"I do believe it was truly an accident. I think she was distracted and being careless as she was trying to figure out what to do." Jenny paused again. "I'm sorry, Hunter. It's like I said, I didn't want to ruin this image you had of her. I thought you could at least hold onto that. I didn't want to be the one to burst your bubble."

His throat burned. How could Stephanie not have talked to him about this?

What else hadn't she told him?

This was a lot for him to think about.

"Thanks for telling me now," Hunter told Jenny. "You did the right thing."

Jenny still sounded unsure as she ended the call.

Hunter gripped his phone and stared in the distance a moment.

It would take a while for that to sink in.

Just as that thought entered his mind, he glanced down the street and saw a delivery truck headed toward the lab.

But before the vehicle reached the building, four men ran from the woods on the opposite side of the road, their guns drawn.

CHAPTER
THIRTY

HUNTER QUICKLY CALLED in the incident—first to Cassidy then to Ocean Essence. He needed to place the building on lockdown.

Then he withdrew his gun and ran toward the scene.

"Hey!"

Unfortunately, the delivery truck had stopped nearly a half mile from the building.

From what Hunter could tell, two men were already in the back of the truck. Another man held the driver at gunpoint while the fourth shooter aimed his gun at Hunter.

A bullet whizzed past him.

He ducked to the ground.

But he was in the middle of a field. There was nowhere to take cover out here.

This wasn't going to work. He was a sitting duck right now.

Backup should be on the way. But it would at least be another five minutes.

He glanced around, looking for the next best plan of action.

Hunter glanced at the gunman and saw the gun was still aimed at him.

Then the man fired another shot.

Raising his own weapon, Hunter squeezed the trigger.

The gunman dove behind the truck.

That gave Hunter the opening he needed to dart toward the woods in the distance.

Just as he reached the tree line, another bullet whizzed by, barely missing him.

He was closer to the truck now, but not close enough to stop these guys.

As he started to move again, a bullet split the wood of the tree beside him.

He ducked back behind the tree.

As he did, he heard talking and yelling in the distance.

He heard doors slam.

What was going on?

He needed a better look.

He fired another shot as cover then, staying low, he ran closer to the truck.

More bullets flew as he dodged around trees. When he got nearer to the road, he hid behind a tree again and glanced out to see what was happening.

The gunmen appeared to be gone.

But the truck was still there, with the driver inside.

Hunter sprinted toward the man, still on guard. "What happened? Are you okay?"

"I'm fine," the driver said. "But those men . . . they grabbed some boxes from the back, and they took off that way." The man nodded toward the woods on the opposite side.

The guys had left the same way they'd arrived.

How had they even gotten here in the first place? He hadn't seen any vehicles pass by on the road before the truck had arrived.

Then Hunter heard a motor.

But it wasn't from a vehicle.

He instantly recognized the familiar sound.

He knew exactly what was happening.

"The police should be here any minute," he told the driver. "Tell them what happened. I'm going after these guys."

The next instant, he took off through the woods on the opposite side of the road. He ran, careful not to trip on the thick underbrush. Branches slapped him as he moved, but he kept up a fast pace.

Just on the other side of this patch of trees was the Pamlico Sound.

He saw glimpses of the water through the trees.

The shoreline was close.

He just needed to clear the woods in time to stop them.

But as he reached the shoreline, he realized he was too late.

The four men were already onboard a boat, zooming through the water and out of reach.

———

"They're not answering!" Panic clawed at Abby as Tali returned upstairs.

Tali had already raced downstairs to tell Mac what was happening.

"Mac's asking the police to check out the theater. We can't think in worst-case scenarios . . . not yet." But Tali couldn't hide the worry in her voice.

Abby feared it was too late. "Someone cloned my phone number. Who knows what other messages they may have sent. We've got to go look for Serena and Cadence!"

Tali frowned. "Let's give it another minute."

"What if they don't have another minute?"

Tali let out a breath before nodding. "Maybe we can catch a ride with Mac. I'm sure he wants to go check this out himself."

Mac was already on his way out the door when they caught up to him.

"The police are apparently tied up with another incident," he explained. "I'm heading over there. Lock the doors when I leave—"

"We're coming with you," Tali interjected, no room for argument in her tone.

Mac paused only for a split second before nodding. "Let's go then."

A few minutes later, they were in his truck and heading down the road.

"Did you say the police were tied up with another incident?" Abby repeated, Mac's words just now hitting her.

"I didn't ask what was happening," Mac said. "No time to waste."

Tali nodded toward the road. "Let's concentrate on finding Serena and Cadence."

"Of course." Abby tried to call Cadence again.

When she didn't answer, her worry grew.

A few minutes later, they pulled up to the theater.

Cadence's car was there.

But when they darted inside the building, it was empty.

Her friends were nowhere to be found.

Just then, her phone rang.

"It's Serena!" Abby answered, putting the phone on speaker.

But it wasn't her friend on the other line. It was a man with a raspy, probably disguised, voice. "I have your friends. I'll trade you. You come with me, and they won't be harmed. Stay tuned for instructions."

"Don't hurt—" Abby began, but it was too late.

The caller had already disconnected.

Abby glanced at Mac and then Tali as she felt fear pulse through her.

This psychopath had her friends.

What was she going to do?

CASSIDY HAD COME to get Hunter's statement fifteen minutes ago.

Several members of the administration at Ocean Essence had come out to question him also. Whatever had been stolen from that truck still wasn't clear to Hunter, but it must have been important if those men had gone through all that trouble to obtain it.

Suddenly, things didn't seem quite as innocent at the lab as they once had. Certainly, there were substances the employees utilized that could be used for things besides cosmetics, things that perhaps in large doses could be deadly or caustic.

Was that why someone had targeted the lab?

Had they stolen something dangerous?

Hunter's jaw tightened at the thought.

He wasn't sure what was going on. He'd have to let Cassidy and her crew figure that out.

As he and Cassidy debriefed, her phone rang. He knew by the way her shoulders tensed that something was wrong. Was it Abby? Had something else happened?

She ended the call and jogged toward her SUV, a new urgency in her steps.

"Cassidy?" He started after her.

She motioned for him to follow her. "Come with me."

He quickly caught up to her and spotted Titus pulling up. "What's going on?"

"There's been another incident." She opened her SUV door and climbed inside, her every motion tense. "Get in."

An incident? Hunter's pulse quickened.

That didn't sound good.

As he rounded the SUV, Hunter motioned to Titus that he would call, and then he climbed into the passenger side of Cassidy's vehicle. He hadn't even finished putting his seatbelt on when she pulled away.

"What's going on?" He grabbed the bar above to brace himself.

Cassidy narrowed her eyes with concern. "Cadence and Serena are missing."

"What?" His pitch rose as he asked the question, uncertain if he'd heard correctly.

"Someone must have cloned Abby's phone and sent the ladies a message that appeared to be from Abby, asking them to meet her at the theater. When Abby realized what had happened, she, Mac, and Tali went to find them, but they were too late."

A throb began at his temples.

Hunter should have never left Abby today. He should have insisted he stay.

But that wouldn't have prevented this from happening. Because, as far as he knew, Abby had been at the bookstore when this unfolded.

Still, he didn't like the scenarios playing out in his mind.

He prayed Cadence and Serena were okay. As he remembered Raef's lifeless body, another round of worry tried to clutch him. He didn't want Cadence and Serena to end up like that.

Please, Lord . . .

"Any leads as to who's behind this?" Hunter stared at the road ahead as his thoughts raced.

Cassidy frowned as she turned down the street leading to the theater. "If I had to guess? It's someone who wants to take away anyone he sees as a threat."

"A threat to what?"

"A threat that will keep Abby from him." Her words sounded solemn.

Hunter wrinkled his forehead, needing to make sure he was understanding her correctly. "What do you mean?"

"I mean, I think someone who's obsessed with Abby may be trying to separate her from everyone and everything she cares about."

Hunter's head spun as realizations hit him like bullets rapid firing into his flesh.

If he were a betting man, he'd put everything on the fact that Cassidy was right.

"An ex-boyfriend?" Abby repeated as she stood outside the theater. "Why would an ex want to isolate me from my friends?"

Her head spun as she tried to process Cassidy's theory.

She leaned against the police SUV. Cassidy was there as well as Mac, Tali, Officer Bradshaw, and . . . Hunter.

Her heart lurched when she saw him. Based on the look in his eyes, he felt the same jolt.

But this wasn't the time to hammer things out between them.

She hoped there might be time for that later.

"That's our working theory, though I'm not sure how CJ fits into it," Cassidy said.

Abby raked a hand through her hair as facts collided in her mind. "Florence—CJ's aunt—told me the other day that CJ had planned on asking me out, but he was trying to gather his nerve."

"There you have it." Cassidy nodded somberly. "This explains why Hunter has been a target also."

Her cheeks heated. But her love life was the least of her concerns right now.

Really, what Abby wanted was for her friends to return unharmed.

She wanted to trade herself for them.

But no one was going to let her do that.

Abby felt beside herself knowing she was here just talking when she should be out there searching for her friends. But she knew that Ty had already arranged for some of his guys at Blackout to scour the island for Cadence and Serena.

Their chances of finding the women were better than hers.

"I think Cassidy is right, Abby." Hunter turned toward her, an intense look in his gaze. "Think about it. You go out on a date with Raef and then he's killed. The theater that you've put so much time and effort and money into is destroyed. The job that you work hard at is compromised. Now, someone has taken your friends away. This guy is stripping away everything important to you."

Abby blinked as she let his words settle. She wanted to argue, but she couldn't.

He was absolutely correct.

Why hadn't she seen this before? It seemed so obvious now.

"Is there anyone in particular you can think of who might be responsible?" Cassidy turned toward Abby, urgency in her gaze.

Abby didn't have to think for very long before answering. "It could be Michael."

"What happened with him again?" Mac shielded his eyes against the afternoon sunlight. "I vaguely remember you mentioning him back at Christmas."

"When I was living in Myrtle Beach, the two of us were working together on a play. He stole some money from the theater and set it up to make me take the blame. None of what was between us was real. He just used me." Abby paused and glanced around at everyone in the circle. Her gaze finally stopped on Cassidy. "You think Michael could have come to Lantern Beach to try to ruin me again?"

Cassidy shrugged. "I'm not 100 percent sure. But it's at least a working theory."

Abby let out a long breath. "Let's say that it's

true. I haven't seen Michael on the island. How would he know CJ wanted to go out with me? How would he know I'd been out with Raef?"

"That's what we need to find out. Maybe we can find out exactly where Michael has been this week," Cassidy said. "That would help to clear this up. Anyone else we should look into?"

"There was Nelson Woods back in Florida," Abby continued. "But he died in a house fire a few months ago."

"We'll look into Michael then," Cassidy said. "What's his last name?"

"LeBlanc."

Cassidy jotted his name down.

"What about Cadence and Serena?" Abby held her breath, hoping for the best. She'd seen Cassidy and Bradshaw glancing at their phones more than once as if they'd gotten messages. "Any updates?"

"Not yet. But I'm going to grab this guy's picture so I can show it around to some people in town. Mac and Bradshaw, you start scouring the area also, see if anyone recognizes Michael LeBlanc." Cassidy glanced at Hunter. "You stay with Abby and Tali."

Hunter looked at Abby as if trying to read her expression before finally nodding. "Will do."

Abby wouldn't argue. Not this time. Not when so much was on the line.

"Mac, can you leave your truck with them and ride with Bradshaw?" Cassidy glanced at the men.

Mac tossed his keys to Hunter. "Of course."

"In the meantime, I can call some old friends and see if they can pinpoint where Michael is," Abby offered, her thoughts racing.

She knew time was of the essence right now, and she didn't want to waste a minute.

"Great idea," Cassidy said. "I'll leave my laptop with you. And Abby, whatever you do, don't you even think about trading yourself for Cadence and Serena. There's a good chance all three of you will be killed if you do. Understand?"

The blood drained from Abby's face, but she nodded.

She didn't like the sound of that.

She only wanted her friends back before it was too late.

ABBY, Tali, and Hunter had climbed inside Mac's truck to wait things out and do some research. There was no time to find another place to go. Not when they could look for answers here as well as anywhere else.

Abby's heart thumped faster with every second that passed as she sat in the front seat next to Hunter.

Hunter had already typed several things into Cassidy's laptop when Tali leaned forward from the backseat. "What can I do?"

"Hang tight for now," Hunter muttered. "I don't see any recent posts on Michael's social media."

"That's unlike him. He's usually boasting all over the internet. Basking in any attention he can get."

"Seems he's vanished from all his socials for the past seven days."

Was that a sign of guilt?

Abby couldn't be certain. But it was definitely something worth considering.

"Is there anybody from Myrtle Beach you can call to ask about him?" Hunter turned toward her.

Seeing him so close to her—and being near enough that she could smell his piney cologne—made her heart ache even more.

But Abby had no one to blame but herself for what had happened between them, and she needed to keep that in mind.

She'd deal with it later.

"There are a couple of people we worked with together on a play," Abby said. "I'm not sure exactly how they would feel about talking to me, but for the sake of this investigation, I can find out."

"If you're comfortable doing that then I do think that it's a good idea."

Abby thought about it a moment before nodding. "Okay then. Let me make a few phone calls."

Her entire life felt like a mess right now.

The idea of going somewhere new and starting over filled her mind again. At least, if Abby did that, she wouldn't have to see Hunter here on the island all the time. She wouldn't have to see the theater that seemed to represent the death of her dreams.

But somehow the thought of leaving Lantern Beach held no appeal at all.

Instead, it left her with a heaviness that was pressing down on her.

Could this all really be happening?

———

Hunter watched as Abby ended her call and frowned. "Well?"

"No one's seen Michael for the past five days," she murmured.

"So that means he could be here in Lantern Beach."

She shrugged. "I suppose. I mean, I don't like to think he's capable of doing something like this."

"But what he did to you back in Myrtle Beach makes it clear he has an unhinged side."

"Yes, but murder? That's a whole other level."

"You never know what someone's truly capable of sometimes . . . until it's too late."

"I suppose you're right." She rubbed a hand over her mouth as if to conceal a frown.

"Does he match this guy's height and build?" Hunter asked.

Abby thought about it a moment. "I guess you

could say that. I mean, I hate to think it could be him. So . . . what do we do now?"

"We let Cassidy know about this development," Tali said. "We can't leave anything to chance. It's not safe to assume anything at this point."

"She's right," Hunter said. "Maybe Cassidy can get a warrant to search his phone records or to see where his phone is pinging from right now. If it shows he's on the island then I suppose we have our answer."

"In the meantime, I'm going to keep asking around." Abby sent messages to more of their mutual friends and anxiously waited to hear back from them.

Meanwhile, she typed Nelson's name into her phone.

Hunter noticed. "I thought you said Nelson was dead."

"He is. But maybe there's a clue somewhere related to Nelson. This could be someone affiliated with him." Abby glanced at Hunter before focusing on her phone screen again. "I'm grasping, I know." She shook her head. "It's probably a dead end, but I have to do something."

Hunter watched as Abby checked Nelson's socials, which were still online. He saw a picture of Nelson with another woman. Just like Abby, she had dark hair, an olive complexion, and was about the same height and build.

Abby clicked on the woman's name and frowned.

"What is it?" Hunter asked.

"This is weird." Abby leaned closer to the screen. "This woman's name is Hannah Larkin. But, according to some news articles, Hannah disappeared about a week before Nelson died."

"What else does it say?" Tali asked.

Abby studied the screen again before she spoke. "In summary, people theorized that she'd taken a long vacation to get away from the stress of her nursing job. But close friends claimed she wouldn't just leave without telling them. She had sent some text messages, but no one had actually talked to her."

"I don't like the sound of that," Hunter muttered.

"I don't either." Abby nibbled on her bottom lip.

"Do you think Nelson did something to her?"

"I don't know what to think anymore." Her voice caught in a sob. "I sure do know how to pick them, don't I?"

Compassion rose in Hunter. He wanted to do something to take away her pain. To comfort her.

But what?

"None of this is your fault," he murmured. "We are doing everything we can to find Serena and Cadence. Cassidy and her team are as well. We just have to give this a little more time. Something will click into place."

Abby still looked unconvinced.

But there was nothing else Hunter could say to reassure her.

ABBY HAD BEEN WAITING for fifteen minutes now to hear back from anyone she'd called or messaged.

So far, there was nothing.

While Hunter stepped outside the truck to make a couple phone calls, she continued researching on the computer, but she hadn't found out any more information.

Tali had mostly remained quiet, as if taking in everything going on around her.

Meanwhile, Cadence and Serena were out there somewhere. Anything could be happening to them right now.

Tension pressed on her chest, and she leaned her head back into the seat.

A moment later, Hunter climbed back into the truck.

He glanced over at her, a new concern in his gaze.

"Find out anything?" Tali asked.

"No. Nothing new." Hunter ran a hand down his face, and then started to reach for Abby's hand but stopped just before touching her.

There were things she wanted to say to Hunter, but she couldn't. Not with Tali here.

It didn't matter anyway. She had more important things to worry about right now.

"Tell me more about this Nelson guy." Hunter leaned back in his seat, his jaw still visibly hardened.

Abby let out a long breath. "His wife had died about a year before we started dating. It soon became clear to me that when he looked at me, he wanted me to be his deceased wife."

Hunter squinted. "You're going to have to explain that a little more."

She told him about the clothing and the perfume.

"That *is* weird," Hunter said.

"When I tried to break up with him, he freaked out. I mean . . . literally freaked out. He shoved me into his bedroom and locked the door from the outside so I couldn't get out."

"What?" Hunter's voice rose.

"He said he couldn't lose me. That he *wouldn't* lose me again."

"Because he was obviously thinking about his wife." Hunter shook his head as he leaned back.

Abby nodded. "It really scared me. I didn't know what he was going to do next."

"How did you get away?" Hunter asked.

"I don't think Nelson had planned on keeping me prisoner—it wasn't premediated. Or if it was, he didn't think things through very well. I was able to open a window and climb out. I ran as fast as I could."

"Oh, sweetheart. That sounds awful." Tali soothed. "Was he arrested?"

Abby nodded. "He was, and he went to a psych hospital for about a week. They said he had a mental break."

Hunter's intense gaze remained on her. "What happened afterward?"

"I never spoke to him again. I . . . couldn't. A few months later he sent me a letter apologizing and explaining how hard losing his wife had been on him. He told me he was getting help and doing a little better."

"I'm glad to hear that, at least."

Abby rubbed her arms as a chill washed over her. "But I guess it still just freaks me out. The whole incident was more traumatic for me than I probably give it credit for."

"I can only imagine," Tali said, her voice soft and gentle.

Before they could talk more, movement in the distance caught Abby's gaze.

She sat up straight and pointed at the woods. "Did you see that?"

"See what?" Hunter bristled.

"Someone's in the woods over there. Watch for a minute. See if he moves again." Abby sucked in a breath. "There. I see a shadow. He's watching us, I think."

His jaw tightened. "Stay here. And call Cassidy. I'm going to find some answers."

With those words, he darted from the vehicle.

———

Hunter sprinted into the woods and froze.

Where had the person gone?

He crept farther into the woods, gun in hand, and listened.

Something shuffled in the brush.

His muscles instantly tightened.

He knew what this was about.

The next person this guy wanted to get rid of was . . . Hunter.

If this madman got his way, Hunter would die, and he could have Abby all to himself.

As he heard something rustling in the brush again, tension rippled across his back.

Someone was playing a game with him right now, and he didn't like it.

A loud sound clattered behind him.

He jerked his head toward the noise.

Nothing was there.

Realization filled him.

That had been a diversion, hadn't it?

Whoever was hiding just out of sight had thrown a rock, hadn't he?

The next instant, someone pounced on his back.

Hunter growled as he felt the man's hand encircle his neck.

This was *not* going to happen.

The guy was smaller than Hunter was, but he was wiry.

This was the same man who'd confronted him in that rental house. Hunter was certain of it.

The guy didn't appear to be giving up.

That was okay because Hunter was in for the fight.

ABBY COULD HARDLY BREATHE AS she waited, her mind racing. "Do you think Hunter is okay?"

"I think he's very capable." But Tali couldn't disguise the worry in her voice as she stared at the woods in the distance also.

Abby's phone rang, and she nearly jumped out of her skin.

She glanced at her screen.

It was Florence. This wasn't the time she wanted to talk about work.

Abby let the call go to voicemail.

But then Florence called again. Maybe it was something important.

With another glance at the woods, Abby reluctantly put the phone to her ear and answered. "Hey,

Florence. This isn't a good time. Can I call you back later?"

"Abby . . ." Her voice quivered. "You're in danger."

Abby's spine straightened at her ominous words. "What do you mean?"

"I met with this man who wanted to buy my cleaning business. He said it was part of his grand plan to start an all-encompassing vacation rental company. Anyway . . . some things happened that raised some red flags."

Abby kept her gaze on the woods as she listened. "Like what?"

"This man . . . he saw your picture in my office and asked who you were. I told him you worked for me. He asked a lot more questions. I just assumed he thought you were pretty."

Various scenarios began to play out in Abby's mind. "Would he have had access to any of the codes?"

"I left him in my office while I went to make copies of some paperwork. I did have a sheet on my desk with an updated list of codes. He could have seen it."

Abby's heart pounded harder. "Florence . . . what did this guy look like?"

"He was handsome. Blond. Fit."

Blond? That didn't fit Michael.

"When this guy saw your picture, I started blabbering like I do sometimes. I told him that my nephew had a crush on you."

Abby's thoughts raced. "Which could be why CJ was attacked . . ."

Florence let out a cry. "Yes, that's what I think also."

She remembered Florence saying earlier that someone had called to check her job reference.

It must have been this psycho. He'd been trying to gather information on her so he could plan his attack.

"Why are you telling me this now?" Abby wondered what had caused her change of heart.

"Because after what happened to CJ, I confronted this guy. I just had this bad feeling he had something to do with it." Her voice cracked. "I don't know what I was thinking—but I was angry. He got violent."

"Oh, Florence . . ."

"He shoved me into the closet at work and locked me there. Another cleaner just stopped by and let me out. I put things together in my mind and realized that this guy was here because of you. I'm worried about you, Abby . . ."

She gripped the phone more tightly as worry pulsed through her. "I'm glad you're okay. I'll let

Cassidy know so she can look for him. She might have some questions for you."

"Of course. Whatever she needs. I'm sorry, Abby. I had no idea this would happen . . . be careful."

"I will be. In the meantime, you stay safe also."

Abby ended the call and glanced back at Tali.

Neither needed to say anything.

They knew exactly what the other was thinking.

Danger was closing in by the moment.

———

Hunter grabbed the man's arms and tried to pull them from around his neck. But his vision blurred.

The guy had a tight grip.

Hunter pivoted and crouched low. In one move, he twisted and flipped the guy over his shoulders and onto the ground in front of him.

The masked man let out a moan.

Shock coursed through Hunter when the guy jumped back to his feet and raised his arms, still ready to fight. Hunter hadn't expected this kind of endurance.

"Where are Cadence and Serena?" Hunter demanded.

"I don't know what you're talking about." Smugness filled the man's words.

"We both know that's not true. Who are you?"

"None of your business."

"Why are you doing this?" Hunter continued to push.

"Isn't it clear?"

"Evidently, it's not."

The man's eyes narrowed. "Stay away from her. She's mine."

His words confirmed to Hunter that Abby was this guy's target. She had been all along.

Raef had most likely been murdered because he'd gone on that date with Abby.

Now this guy was targeting Hunter as well.

The man let out a guttural yell before charging at Hunter.

The action threw Hunter off guard, and the man tackled him to the ground. At once, the guy straddled Hunter and began throwing punches at his face.

It only took a moment for Hunter to come to his senses, to block the hits.

He had to put himself in a better position. This man had too much power right now.

Hunter grabbed the man's arm and twisted it until the guy closed his eyes with pain.

The next instant, Hunter flipped him, and the man hit the ground.

Hunter started to reach for the man's mask, to discover once and for all who was behind all of this.

Before he could, sirens sounded.

Suddenly, the man flung his hand toward Hunter. Something hit Hunter's eyes.

Sand, he realized. The man had grabbed sand and threw it at him.

He lunged back as his eyes began to burn. Blinking, he tried to clear his gaze so he could see what the guy would do next.

But in that brief period, the man ran back into the brush.

Disappeared.

Hunter couldn't let this guy get away. Not when he'd been so close to discovering his identity and stopping him.

He blinked several more times, trying to get the sandy grains from his eyes.

But it was no use. He needed to flush them out.

Despite that, he lumbered toward the trees. Maybe he would go after him anyway.

Before he could, Cassidy pulled up.

"He went that way." Hunter pointed to the woods.

Cassidy took off in a run to try to catch the guy.

CHAPTER
THIRTY-FIVE

EVEN THOUGH ABBY was supposed to stay put, she was certain the danger was long gone. She could barely see what had happened at the edge of the woods—but she'd seen enough.

Then Cassidy had arrived and sprinted into the woods. She must be chasing the guy.

Based on the way Hunter blinked and bent over, something—or a lot of somethings—had gotten into his eyes.

Abby needed to get to Hunter. To see he was okay with her own eyes. She needed to know what had happened.

Making a split-second decision, she slipped out of the truck and ran toward him.

She wanted to touch him. Pull him into a hug. To cover his face with her hands.

Instead, when she reached him, she paused.

Her heart caught her in her throat as she studied him, as she saw the pain he was in. "Are you okay?"

He squinted and shook his head. "That guy . . . he ran into the woods."

"Cassidy went after him. Maybe she'll catch him soon."

"Abby . . . that man, he said . . . that I should stay away . . . that you were his."

A chill washed through her.

That meant that Hunter had almost gotten killed because of her.

There was no denying it now.

She was the center of all this.

That thought didn't sit well with her.

Her earlier inclinations about getting off this island seemed like a better and better idea all the time. The more people she was in contact with, the more people who would be in danger. Abby couldn't live with herself if something happened to one of her friends because of her.

An ache formed in her chest at the thought of it.

An ache also formed at the thought of leaving the island and everyone she cared about behind.

What was she going to do?

Just then, she heard the rustling in the woods again.

The brush was too thick. She couldn't see who might be there.

Was it Cassidy?

Her heart pounded harder.

Or was it the madman who wanted to kill everyone close to her.

———

Hunter bristled when he heard the sound, and he pushed himself in front of Abby.

A moment later, Cassidy appeared from between the trees.

She wore a scowl.

"I told you to stay in the car." She threw Abby a pointed look.

"I knew the bad guy was gone, and I needed to check on Hunter," she rushed.

Cassidy gave her another look before glancing back at Hunter.

He'd stopped blinking as much, but he still needed some saline solution for his eyes.

"He got away. I don't even know where he went, but he's gone." Cassidy peered closer at Hunter. "Let me get an eye kit from my SUV."

She jogged toward her vehicle and reappeared a few minutes later with something in her hands.

After flushing his eyes, most of the debris was finally cleared.

Hunter blinked several times and used the edge of his shirt to wipe his eyes.

In all his years of being a Navy SEAL and fighting for this country, no one had ever thrown sand into his eyes before. This was a new experience he didn't want to repeat.

"What now?" Hunter straightened. "Should your guys keep looking for him?"

"I have a feeling this guy is a chameleon and that he's disappeared." Cassidy scowled. "By the time backup gets here, he's going to be long gone."

Hunter wanted to argue, but he couldn't. He knew her words were true. The PD was already spread thin as they searched for Cadence and Serena.

But that didn't mean he liked it.

"Florence called," Abby rushed.

She told Hunter what the woman had said, and more pieces clicked in place.

Cassidy jotted down some notes.

"What do you want me to do?" Hunter ran a hand over his eyes one more time as he felt a new determination settle over him.

"I need Abby and Tali to be safe," Cassidy continued. "Take them to the station and wait there with them until I get back. Okay?"

Hunter nodded. "Yes, ma'am."

CHAPTER
THIRTY-SIX

ABBY'S THOUGHTS continued to race as she, Hunter, and Tali headed down the road toward the police station.

Just as before, it seemed a shame to be sitting here when she could be out there helping to find her friends. But what else was she supposed to do?

Cassidy was right. Abby was a target. And she didn't want to do anything that would get in the way of the search for her friends.

But there was so much she wanted to say and do.

So much she wanted to say to Hunter.

What if she didn't get that opportunity?

As if extending an olive branch, he reached over and squeezed her hand.

He didn't say anything.

He didn't have to.

Abby squeezed his hand in return and held on tight, almost feeling as if the touch were a lifeline.

She had to keep her hopes alive that her friends would be found. That this man—Michael?—would be arrested. That everything would be okay.

"Where could he have taken them?" Abby murmured as her thoughts raced.

"If he had the access codes to rental houses, what if he stashed them inside one?"

Abby sucked in a breath. "That makes a lot of sense. He very well *could* have done that. Maybe I should call Cassidy."

"It's a good idea," Hunter confirmed.

She quickly dialed the police chief's number and gave her the update.

Just as Abby ended the call, a squeal sounded close by.

The next moment, a car slammed into the front of the truck.

The sudden impact jerked Abby forward, and everything around her blurred.

———

Hunter forced his eyes open.

Reality slammed into his mind.

A vehicle had rammed the truck.

He blinked, trying to ignore the ringing in his ears.

He glanced at Abby and saw that she was beginning to stir.

He didn't see any obvious injuries.

He turned to look at Tali. His breath caught.

She appeared to be unconscious in the back seat.

No . . .

As he unbuckled his seatbelt so he could check on Tali, a movement in front of him drew his attention.

The masked driver was climbing out of the car that had hit them.

Hunter knew exactly what this guy wanted.

The man was coming for Abby.

Hunter had to stop him before he reached her.

Quickly, he grabbed his gun and stepped out of the truck. He stood, his legs—and head—wobbling a moment. He quickly righted himself and ran around the vehicle toward Abby's door.

As he did, the man disappeared.

Where had he gone?

The hair on the back of Hunter's neck stood on end.

He whirled around.

But he was too late.

An electric pulse hit him.

Stunned, Hunter fell to his knees, then collapsed onto the pavement.

Another Taser. The man had gotten him with a Taser again.

Hunter tried to right himself, but it was no use.

He had to wait for the shock to wear off.

He watched as the man stood over him.

The guy was no longer wearing a mask.

Nor was his hair blond.

He must have been wearing a wig when he'd met with Florence.

Hunter's thoughts raced as he tried to regain control of his limbs.

This man wasn't Michael. Hunter was sure of that.

But an aura of danger surrounded this guy.

If he took Abby, there was a good chance no one would ever see her again.

Hunter couldn't let that happen.

He tried to move. To fight. To protect Abby.

But the Taser had rendered him immobile.

He was at this man's mercy.

Or lack thereof.

ABBY FELT panic racing through her as Hunter exited the truck.

"Tali . . ." Abby glanced at the back seat.

Tali didn't respond.

She couldn't.

She had passed out.

Her eyes were closed.

She looked pale.

But she was alive.

Abby only knew that because she'd seen the rise and fall of Tali's chest.

Dear Lord, help her. Help all of us.

As Hunter approached her side of the truck, she saw the gun in his hand as he looked around.

Where had that man who'd hit them gone? Abby had seen him step out. But now he'd disappeared.

Panic raced through her.

The next instant, Hunter spun around and a buzzing sound filled the air.

He fell to the ground.

No . . . !

Then Abby saw the man standing over Hunter.

Without his mask.

The six-foot-tall man with his short, dark hair. With his hooded gaze. His lean but muscular frame.

And his eyes . . . which made it clear something was off.

Abby's stomach dropped. Her pulse galloped. She sucked in quick, erratic breaths.

All her nightmares seemed to be coming to fruition at once.

Nelson.

He was alive.

And he'd found her here in Lantern Beach.

The delusional man still wanted what was his—and he considered Abby his property.

A deep fear filled her chest at the implications of what he might do next.

With a gleam in his eyes, Nelson pulled out his gun and aimed it at Hunter. "I won't hurt him if you come with me. Abby, open the door and get out. We don't have any time to waste."

Her limbs trembled as she unlocked and cracked

open the door. She didn't know what to do. She couldn't let him hurt Hunter, but she also couldn't get out and go with Nelson.

She needed to buy some time. Someone else would come down this road eventually. They'd find them.

Be able to help.

Or they could become another victim.

No . . . Lord, please let a cop come this way. Not another innocent bystander.

And be with Tali. Help her be okay. Please, I'm begging You.

"I thought you were dead." Her voice quivered as she stared at Nelson.

"I had to fake my death. The authorities thought I might have caused Hannah's disappearance."

Abby swallowed hard. "Did you?"

"It wasn't my fault. I didn't want to hurt her. But she tried to kill me."

The only reason she would have tried to kill Nelson was in self-defense. Abby felt certain of that.

A knot formed in her throat. "What happened to her?"

"She was going to leave me." His nostrils flared. "She swore she wasn't when I confronted her. But I always knew when she tried to lie to me. She wasn't very good at it."

"What did you do to her?"

"I just tried to talk some sense into her. But she wouldn't listen. She had to have her way. She always had to have her way. I had to show her she was wrong. I squeezed her neck a little too hard. The next thing I knew . . . she stopped breathing." Veins popped out at his temples as he seemed to relive the moment. "She was dead."

"What happened next?" Abby didn't really want to know, but she needed to buy some time. Give Hunter a chance to recuperate. "What did you do with her?"

"I threw her body into the bay."

"And whose body did they find in the house? The one investigators thought was you?"

"Hannah's ex-boyfriend. He came to my place and got rough with me. I had to strangle him too . . ." His voice caught. "I had no other choice."

"Nelson . . . you always have a choice. Even right now."

His eyes narrowed. "And so do you. Get out of the vehicle."

When she didn't do it right away, he shoved his gun closer to Hunter.

"Now!" Spittle flew from his mouth.

Abby barely got the door open wide enough to exit. She didn't even feel like she was in control of her own body right now. Instead, fear dictated her every action.

As she stood, she held onto the door, unsure if her legs would hold her up.

"You look just as beautiful as you always have, my Kimberly." Nelson's voice softened. "I'm sorry things had to go this way."

Her fear deepened at his words.

Kimberly had been his wife.

He'd slipped up and called Abby by his wife's name a couple of times when they'd been dating. She tried to dismiss it, thinking it had been a mistake.

But clearly there had been warning signs she'd ignored. If only she could go back . . .

She glanced at Hunter, and his haggard gaze met hers.

He was sending her a silent message.

A message not to listen to anything Nelson said.

But if it came down to a choice between his life or hers, then the decision was going to be easy.

She wouldn't let others suffer for her mistakes.

Not if she could help it.

———

Hunter felt himself slowly regaining control of his arms and legs. But he didn't want this guy to know that.

Nelson had been behind this the whole time.

The way he referred to Abby by a different name was just eerie. It made Hunter sick to his stomach.

But he was also aware of the gun pointed directly at his temple.

He'd dropped his own gun when the Taser hit him. It had fallen onto the road probably a good four feet away.

Out of reach.

The guy had obviously escalated his methods from strangulation to using a gun.

He must be getting desperate.

That or he'd grown vengeful.

He wanted Hunter to be out of Abby's life. For good.

Hunter couldn't let him succeed.

"Don't hurt Hunter." Abby's voice quivered.

"I won't." Nelson's voice sounded tight, almost as if his adrenaline and delusions had overcome him. "Not if you come with me quietly."

Abby's trepid gaze met Hunter's before sliding back to Nelson. "Where are we going to go?"

"Somewhere we can start a new life. I was thinking about when we took our honeymoon in Mexico. It would be nice to go back there and start over, wouldn't it? We could build a new life for ourselves. Just you and me. Together. What do you think?"

"Nelson . . . you know that wasn't me on that trip. That was Kimberly on your honeymoon."

"You *are* Kimberly." His words came out crisp and almost harsh.

Hunter didn't know whether Abby correcting him was a good idea or not. Maybe she should play his game for now.

But Hunter wasn't sure the best method.

He only knew he needed to keep her alive.

He couldn't fail her like he'd failed Stephanie.

"I need you to come with me," Nelson growled, his anger rising. "We don't have much time."

"You don't even have a car to drive." Abby nodded at his vehicle. "You crashed it."

"I have another one hiding in the woods. You're coming with me. Or your boyfriend here will pay the price."

Abby glanced at Hunter again, and he knew exactly what she was thinking.

She was going to listen to this guy's demands to save Hunter.

But he couldn't let her do that.

He had to do something.

And whatever it was, Hunter had to do it fast.

CHAPTER
THIRTY-EIGHT

ABBY'S THOUGHTS RACED.

She had to figure out how to get out of this situation.

She needed a way to keep her friends safe.

But none of the answers seemed clear right now.

She glanced at Hunter one more time, and her heart ached.

She knew by the look in Nelson's eyes that he wouldn't hesitate to pull the trigger.

She couldn't let him do that. Not if she had the power to intercede. To end this mess.

There was only one solution.

"I'll go with you," Abby finally said.

"Abby . . . no." The words left Hunter's throat in a hoarse moan.

"You're a smart woman," Nelson said. "I've always known you were. So brilliant. I knew from the moment I met you that the two of us were meant to be together . . . forever."

He was delusional right now. Caught up in some type of fantasy where his wife hadn't died.

Abby could only imagine his grief. Part of her did feel sorry for him.

But this wasn't the way he should go about it.

Maybe Abby could use his misconception to her advantage.

Maybe if she left with him, she could play along until she figured out a way to escape. If she gained his trust, then eventually she might be able to sneak away and get to safety. And she could call the police.

Then Hunter and Tali would both be alive still.

That was it. It was the only plan that would work. The only way to have any power in this situation.

Abby stepped farther from the car, skirting around Hunter. She tried to send him the silent message that she was sorry. About everything. About overreacting when she'd gotten that photo. Of letting past hurts cloud her judgment.

He stared back at her, also sending his own message.

The message not to go with this guy.

Abby wouldn't if she had any other choice.

She reached out her hand, almost as a peace offering toward Nelson. He still held the gun with one hand, but he took her fingers between his with the other.

"I'm so glad to have you back," he murmured, his entire demeanor softening. "You can't even imagine how happy that makes me, my sweet Kimberly."

As his fingers tightened, Abby knew there was no turning back now.

She had to believe she was doing the right thing.

———

Hunter was beginning to be able to move again.

But he didn't want Nelson to know.

Not yet.

But there was no way Abby could leave with this guy.

He knew why she had agreed—for his sake.

There was no way he'd let her sacrifice herself for him.

Nelson took a step back, still facing Hunter, gun still drawn. His other hand still gripping Abby's.

The man wasn't taking any chances.

But the look on Abby's face . . . it was pure terror.

She hardly looked like she was breathing. But he also saw the resignation in her gaze.

Nelson took a few more steps before he finally turned his back on Hunter.

That was Hunter's sign to act.

He leapt to his feet, praying for a steadiness he wasn't sure he had. Either way, he had to push through this.

There wouldn't be any second chances.

He lunged toward the man.

He hit the man's shoulders and tackled him to the ground.

The man let out a guttural yell as he turned toward Hunter.

The crazy look in Nelson's eyes let Hunter know this would be a fight for his life.

"Run!" he yelled to Abby.

Her eyes widened as she stepped back.

But she didn't flee.

Instead, a determined look entered her eyes.

Before Hunter could say anything else, Nelson had an almost feral burst of energy.

He flipped Hunter onto his back and growled, showing his teeth.

Hunter glanced to the side.

Saw Nelson's gun on the ground.

If he could only grab it . . .

But Nelson saw the weapon at the same time.

Whoever grabbed it first would most likely be the sole survivor, Hunter realized.

He had to reach it before Nelson did.

ABBY SAW everything unfold and felt a rush of panic sweep through her.

Hunter and Nelson thrashed on the ground.

Hunter reached for the weapon.

Before he could touch it, Nelson jammed his knee into Hunter's gut.

No . . .

Why was she letting fear paralyze her? No more excuses. She'd used them for far too long.

She couldn't let Nelson get that gun.

Abby lunged toward the weapon.

Just as the tips of Nelson's fingers touched the gun, Abby snatched it.

Her hands shook as she gripped the gun and raised it.

But the two men were moving so much that she

wasn't sure who she was aiming at. She couldn't get a clear aim on Nelson.

Instead, Abby raised it in the air and fired a warning shot.

The recoil reverberated in her hand. Traveled up her arm.

She didn't like guns. Didn't like firing them.

But she'd do it again if she needed to.

The men stopped fighting and stared at her.

Then she pointed the gun at Nelson. "Get up."

"Kimberly . . ." His tone held warning, as if he were putting Abby in her place and reminding her to be submissive.

"My name is Abby, and I said get up." Her voice sounded stronger than she felt. Maybe her acting skills were coming in handy.

Maybe.

But this could all backfire.

"You and I are meant to be together," Nelson muttered. "You know that. We talked about it."

"Your wife died of an aneurism," Abby reminded him, compassion creeping into her tone. But she had to remind him of the truth. "She's gone."

"No . . ." His face reddened.

"You know it's true. Where did you leave my friends, Nelson?" Abby demanded. "Where are they?"

His eyes brightened. "If you come with me, I'll tell you, and you can call whoever you want. I'm sorry it has to be this way."

"No, you're not. You're trying to manipulate me." Abby's voice quivered.

"I'm not, Kimberly. I'd do anything for you. I just want you."

"And you'll do anything to get that, won't you?" Disgust filled her.

At once, Hunter swept his legs under Nelson's feet.

The man fell to the ground.

When he did, Hunter grabbed Nelson's arms and twisted them behind his back.

Abby watched, waiting for the other shoe to drop.

But Nelson couldn't fight back.

Hunter had subdued him.

She drew in quick, raspy breaths as she waited.

Could this really be over?

She held her hopes at bay.

She'd seen situations go south too many times.

———

A few minutes later, police and paramedics arrived on the scene.

Hunter released his breath as Cassidy hopped

from her car and rushed to arrest Nelson. Mac went straight for Tali, who'd begun to stir.

Hunter released his breath as he realized this was finally over.

Almost.

He glanced at Abby who still stood there, gun in her trembling hand.

Carefully, Hunter stepped toward her. "It's okay. It's over now. Give me the gun."

Abby's gaze flickered up to meet his.

Shock mixed with panic in her eyes, and she remained frozen.

"Abby . . ." He took a cautious step closer. "It's okay. It's over."

He'd seen people react in unexpected ways during times of stress.

He didn't want to take any chances now.

Abby's gaze met his again, and her shoulders softened ever so slightly.

"I'm going to take the gun from you, okay?" he coaxed her. "Take your finger off the trigger."

It took her a minute, but Abby finally released her grip.

"I'm going to slide it out of your hand," Hunter continued.

She remained frozen as he took the Glock from her hands. He emptied the chamber before shoving the gun into his waistband.

Not missing a beat, he pulled Abby into his arms.

She fell into his embrace, nuzzling herself into his chest.

Holding her close had never felt so good.

But, just as quickly as Abby relaxed, she stiffened again. "What about Cadence and Serena?"

"We found them." Cassidy stepped closer. "You were right. They'd been locked in a pantry at one of the rental houses. They're fine."

Her muscles softened. "And Tali? Is she okay? She wasn't moving last time I saw her."

"She's fine," Cassidy said. "Paramedics are checking her out, but her vitals are all good."

Hunter glanced back and saw Tali standing next to Mac, who had a protective arm around her.

"I'm not letting her out of my sight for a long time to come," Mac assured them.

At those words, Abby buried herself deeper in Hunter's chest.

Hunter held tight, refusing to let go.

Maybe they could finally put this all behind them.

As Cassidy stuffed Nelson in the back of the police cruiser, the man took one more stab at Abby. "This isn't the end of things! We're meant to be together, Kimberly. Nothing will ever change my mind about that! I'll come for you again. I'll never stop coming for you."

"You're wrong," Hunter spoke up. "You'll never get near her again."

Nelson would be going away for a long time. Hunter felt certain of it.

Abby was finally safe, and that was something he could truly be thankful for.

FOUR HOURS LATER, Abby and Hunter returned to the bookstore.

Hunter unlocked the door—Mac had given them a spare key—and let them inside.

But they didn't hurry upstairs. Instead, they sat on a couch tucked in the corner.

Tali and Mac had arrived earlier, and they were both already upstairs in the apartment.

Thankfully, Cadence and Serena were found unharmed—just frightened.

Abby was so grateful they were okay. She'd been so worried.

She'd already spoken to each of them on the phone, and she'd told them she'd catch up with them later.

For now, she had a lot she wanted to tell Hunter.

"I'm sorry I pushed you away," she started, ignoring the lump in her throat. "I guess after everything that happened with Nelson and Michael, I freaked out."

"It's okay." He shrugged. "I didn't know what you'd been through."

"I didn't have a chance to show you this yet." She found the photos in her text messages and handed the device to him.

His eyes widened when he saw the picture of him and Stephanie.

"What?" he muttered.

"Nelson must have found them somehow."

"I guess so. And he sent them to you . . ." He frowned. "Abby . . . you have to know that I'm not thinking of you as a replacement for Stephanie."

"I know," she rushed. "But my mind automatically went to the worst-case scenario. I guess I just kind of freaked out, and I want to say I'm sorry."

"It's okay. I'm glad you told me. I know what you went through with him must've been traumatic."

"He was far more twisted than I thought he was."

"He definitely needs professional help," Hunter agreed.

Abby leaned into Hunter's embrace, finding immense comfort in his arms.

He pulled her close. "I just found out that Stephanie actually had a gambling problem."

She lifted her head in surprise. "What?"

"I knew something was going on. I just didn't know what. The truth is, I always felt like I'd failed her—in more ways than one. I don't want to fail you also."

She reached up and stroked his beard. "I don't think that's even a possibility. We are two imperfect people. I'm sure we'll make mistakes. But the key is rising above them. Together."

Hunter grinned. "I like that. Are you still thinking about leaving?"

She shook her head. "No. My mom taught me that running was the answer. But I'm an adult now and my own woman. I don't want to follow in her footsteps. And it's my choice not to. I've come to realize that something in the past keeps whispering in our ears, even when we tell it to be quiet."

"That sounds poetic."

She let out a feeble laugh. "I guess it does. But it's really not. Sometimes, those whispers can feel tragic."

"I understand. But, on a positive note, I'm glad you're staying."

"Are you?" Abby raised her eyebrows. "And why is that?"

"So I can do this every single day." With those words, Hunter leaned closer and placed his lips on hers.

———

The next morning, Cassidy asked Hunter and Abby to meet her at the station.

Hunter was anxious to hear what she had to say.

Cassidy looked tired when she greeted them. She took a sip of her coffee and directed them to sit down.

"How are you both doing this morning?" Cassidy started.

"Glad this is over," Abby admitted.

"We all are. I don't think you have to worry about Nelson anymore. I have a feeling he's going to be locked up for a long time."

"We hope so." Hunter squeezed Abby's hand reassuringly.

"In other news, I heard from one of my colleagues in Myrtle Beach that Michael has been found."

Abby stiffened. "Is he . . . alive?"

"He is. Apparently, Nelson tried to attack him, but he got away. He went into hiding. Police tracked him down at a local hotel and gave him the update."

"That's good news."

"And . . ." Cassidy paused. "I had a phone call this morning about the theater."

Abby straightened in her chair. "What about it?"

"Unfortunately, the building itself probably won't be done in time for opening night. However . . . we've had a donor step up and offer to build an outdoor amphitheater on the theater grounds."

"What?" Surprise laced Abby's voice.

Cassidy nodded slowly. "That's right. They think it will be faster. They said you can ask people to bring their own beach chairs or camping chairs to set on the lawn."

"Wow . . . that's so generous."

Cassidy nodded again, but she didn't look overly enthusiastic. Why was that? Hunter wondered.

"I thought you'd want to know," Cassidy finished.

"Absolutely. Thank you so much."

"You can hash out the details later."

After talking for a few more minutes, they stood. But before Hunter left, he had one more question on his mind. "Any update on that robbery at Ocean Essence?"

Cassidy's gaze darkened. "I spent some time this morning before you got here trying to find answers. I'm afraid I'm getting the runaround."

"What do you mean?"

"Between us, the CEO said he believes it was rubbing alcohol that was stolen, but they're still trying to check their invoices to confirm that."

"Why would armed robbers steal rubbing alcohol?"

"My thoughts exactly. Personally, I have to wonder if it was some other chemical—something they don't advertise as using in their products since the company claims to be chemical free. If that's true, and if news of that leaked to the public . . . it wouldn't be good for Ocean Essence."

"There are a lot of substances that could be dangerous," Hunter finished.

She nodded grimly. "That's why I have to get to the bottom of this. I told them they had until the end of the day to give me a more definitive answer. Dr. Frank Hensley, the CEO, didn't like that. But if there's some kind of coverup going on at the company, I need to know about it."

"Absolutely." Hunter nodded. "If there's anything I can help you with, let me know."

"I just might do that. Thanks. Now, you two go and relax some. It's been a long week, hasn't it?"

"It sure has," Abby murmured. When they stepped out of the office and closed the door, she added, "So, I guess this means you're not my body-guard anymore?"

"I will always protect you. But I don't just mean physically." Hunter turned toward her and lowered his voice as he leaned close. "I promise I'll also always protect your heart."

A warm sensation filled her, and she wrapped her arms around Hunter. "Is that right?"

"That's right. I *am* a trained professional, after all." His eyes sparkled.

Abby smiled as she seemed to remember reciting those same words to him. "In that case, I trust you."

He planted a soft kiss on her lips. "Those words mean the world to me."

"And I can't wait for you to bake a batch of those chocolate chip cookies for me sometime."

He chuckled. "I'll have you know, I don't make cookies for just anyone. But I'd be more than happy to make them for you anytime."

"You sure do know the way to a girl's heart. And to think, it wasn't that long ago that I was convinced fairy tale endings only existed onstage." Abby grinned as she reached up and planted another kiss on his lips.

~~~

Thank you for reading **Shattered Whispers**. If you enjoyed this book, please consider leaving a review.
~~~

Stay tuned for ***Unsteady Ground,*** coming next!

ALSO BY CHRISTY BARRITT:

OTHER BOOKS IN THE LANTERN BEACH SERIES:

LANTERN BEACH MYSTERIES

Hidden Currents

You can take the detective out of the investigation, but you can't take the investigator out of the detective. A notorious gang puts a bounty on Detective Lady Matthews's head after she takes down their leader, leaving her no choice but to hide until she can testify at trial. But her temporary home across the country on a remote North Carolina island isn't as peaceful as she initially thinks. Living under the new identity of Cassidy Livingston, she struggles to keep her investigative skills tucked away, especially after a body washes ashore. When local police bungle the murder investigation, she can't resist stepping in. But Cassidy is supposed to be keeping a low profile. One wrong move could lead to both her discovery and her demise. Can she bring justice to the island . . . or will the hidden currents surrounding her pull her under for good?

Flood Watch

The tide is high, and so is the danger on Lantern Beach. Still in hiding after infiltrating a dangerous gang, Cassidy Livingston just has to make it a few more months before she can testify at trial and resume her old life. But trouble keeps finding her, and Cassidy is pulled into a local investigation after a man mysteriously disappears from the island she now calls home. A recurring nightmare from her time undercover only muddies things, as does a visit from the parents of her handsome ex-Navy SEAL neighbor. When a friend's life is threatened, Cassidy must make choices that put her on the verge of blowing her cover. With a flood watch on her emotions and her life in a tangle, will Cassidy find the truth? Or will her past finally drown her?

Storm Surge

A storm is brewing hundreds of miles away, but its effects are devastating even from afar. Laid-back, loose, and light: that's Cassidy Livingston's new motto. But when a makeshift boat with a bloody cloth inside washes ashore near her oceanfront home, her detective instincts shift into gear . . . again. Seeking clues isn't the only thing on her mind—romance is heating up with next-door neighbor and former Navy SEAL Ty Chambers as well. Her heart wants the love and stability she's longed for her entire life. But her hidden identity only leads to a tidal wave of turbulence. As more answers emerge about the boat, the danger around her rises, creating a treacherous swell that threatens to reveal her past. Can Cassidy mind her own business, or will the storm surge of violence and corruption that has washed ashore on Lantern Beach leave her life in wreckage?

Dangerous Waters

Danger lurks on the horizon, leaving only two choices: find shelter or flee. Cassidy Livingston's new identity has begun to feel as comfortable as her favorite sweater. She's been tucked away on Lantern Beach for weeks, waiting to testify against a deadly gang, and is settling in to a new life she wants to last forever. When she thinks she spots someone malevolent from her past, panic swells inside her. If an enemy has found her, Cassidy won't be the only one who's a target. Everyone she's come to love will also be at risk. Dangerous waters threaten to pull her into an overpowering chasm she may never escape. Can

Cassidy survive what lies ahead? Or has the tide fatally turned against her?

Perilous Riptide

Just when the current seems safer, an unseen danger emerges and threatens to destroy everything. When Cassidy Livingston finds a journal hidden deep in the recesses of her ice cream truck, her curiosity kicks into high gear. Islanders suspect that Elsa, the journal's owner, didn't die accidentally. Her final entry indicates their suspicions might be correct and that what Elsa observed on her final night may have led to her demise. Against the advice of Ty Chambers, her former Navy SEAL boyfriend, Cassidy taps into her detective skills and hunts for answers. But her search only leads to a skeletal body and trouble for both of them. As helplessness threatens to drown her, Cassidy is desperate to turn back time. Can Cassidy find what she needs to navigate the perilous situation? Or will the riptide surrounding her threaten everyone and everything Cassidy loves?

Deadly Undertow

The current's fatal pull is powerful, but so is one detective's will to live. When someone from Cassidy Livingston's past shows up on Lantern Beach and warns her of impending peril, opposing currents collide, threatening to drag her under. Running would be easy. But leaving would break her heart. Cassidy must decipher between the truth and lies, between reality and deception. Even more importantly, she must decide whom to trust and whom to fear. Her life depends on it. As danger rises and answers surface, everything Cassidy thought she knew is tested. In order to survive, Cassidy must take drastic measures and end the battle against the ruthless gang DH-7 once and for all. But if her final mission fails, the consequences will be as deadly as the raging undertow.

LANTERN BEACH ROMANTIC SUSPENSE

Tides of Deception

Change has come to Lantern Beach: a new police chief, a new season, and . . . a new romance? Austin Brooks has loved Skye Lavinia from the moment they met, but the walls she keeps around her seem impenetrable. Skye knows Austin is the best thing to ever happen to her. Yet she also knows that if he learns the truth about her past, he'd be a fool not to run. A chance encounter brings secrets bubbling to the surface, and danger soon follows. Are the life-threatening events plaguing them really accidents . . . or is someone trying to send a deadly message? With the tides on Lantern Beach come deception and lies. One question remains—who will be swept away as the water shifts? And will it bring the end for Austin and Skye, or merely the beginning?

Shadow of Intrigue

For her entire life, Lisa Garth has felt like a supporting character in the drama of life. The designation never bothered her—until now. Lantern Beach, where she's settled and runs a popular restaurant, has boarded up for the season. The slower pace leaves her with too much time alone. Braden Dillinger came to Lantern Beach to try to heal. The former Special Forces officer returned from battle with invisible scars and diminished hope. But his recovery is hampered by the fact that an unknown enemy is trying to kill him. From the moment Lisa and Braden meet, danger ignites around them, and both are drawn into a web of intrigue that turns their lives upside down. As shadows creep in, will Lisa and Braden be able to shine a light on the peril around them? Or will the encroaching darkness turn their worst nightmares into reality?

Storm of Doubt

A pastor who's lost faith in God. A romance

writer who's lost faith in love. A faceless man with a deadly obsession. Nothing has felt right in Pastor Jack Wilson's world since his wife died two years ago. He hoped coming to Lantern Beach might help soothe the ragged edges of his soul. Instead, he feels more alone than ever. Novelist Juliette Grace came to the island to hide away. Though her professional life has never been better, her personal life has imploded. Her husband left her and a stalker's threats have grown more and more dangerous. When Jack saves Juliette from an attack, he sees the terror in her gaze and knows he must protect her. But when danger strikes again, will Jack be able to keep her safe? Or will the approaching storm prove too strong to withstand?

Winds of Danger

Wes O'Neill is perfectly content to hang with his friends and enjoy island life on Lantern Beach. Something begins to change inside him when Paige Henderson sweeps into his life. But the beautiful newcomer is hiding painful secrets beneath her cheerful facade. Police dispatcher Paige Henderson came to Lantern Beach riddled with guilt and uncertainties after the fallout of a bad relationship. When she meets Wes, she begins to open up to the possibility of love again. But there's something Wes isn't telling her—something that could change everything. As the winds shift, doubts seep into Paige's mind. Can Paige and Wes trust each other, even as the currents work against them? Or is trouble from the past too much to overcome?

Rains of Remorse

A stranger invades her home, leaving Rebecca Jarvis terrified. Above all, she must protect the baby growing inside her. Since her estranged husband died suspiciously six months earlier, Rebecca has been determined to depend on no one but herself. Her chivalrous new neighbor appears to be an answer to prayer. But who is Levi Stoneman really? Rebecca wants to believe he can help her, but she can't ignore her instincts. As danger closes in, both Rebecca and Levi must figure out whom they can trust. With Rebecca's baby coming soon, there's no time to waste. Can the truth prevail . . . or will remorse overpower the best of intentions?

Torrents of Fear

The woman lingering in the crowd can't be Allison . . . can she? Because Allison was pronounced dead six years ago. Musician Carter Denver knows only one person who's capable of helping him find answers: Sadie Thompson, his estranged best friend and someone who also knew Allison. He needs to know if he's losing his mind or if Allison could have survived her car accident. Could Allison really be alive? If so, why is she trying to harm Carter and Sadie? As the two try to find answers, can Sadie keep her feelings for Carter hidden? Could he ever care for her, or is the man of her dreams still in love with the woman now causing his nightmares?

LANTERN BEACH PD

On the Lookout

A runaway woman. A dead body. A mysterious compound. When Cassidy Chambers accepted the job as police chief on Lantern Beach, she knew the island had its secrets. But a suspicious death with potentially far-reaching implications will test all her skills—and threaten to reveal her true identity. Cassidy enlists the help of her husband, former Navy SEAL Ty Chambers. As they dig for answers, both uncover parts of their pasts that are best left buried. Not everything is as it seems, and they must figure out if their John Doe is connected to the secretive group that has moved onto the island. As facts materialize, danger on the island grows. Can Cassidy and Ty discover the truth about the shadowy crimes in their cozy community? Or has darkness permanently invaded their beloved Lantern Beach?

Attempt to Locate

A fun girls' night out turns into a nightmare when armed robbers barge into the store where Cassidy and her friends are shopping. As the situation escalates and the men escape, a massive manhunt launches on Lantern Beach to apprehend the dangerous trio. In the midst of the chaos, a potential foe asks for Cassidy's help. He needs to find his sister who fled from the secretive Gilead's Cove community on the island. But the more Cassidy learns about the seemingly untouchable group, the more her unease grows. The pressure to solve both cases continues to mount. But as the gravity of the situation rises, so does the danger. Cassidy is determined to protect the island and break up the cult . . . but doing so might cost her everything.

First Degree Murder

Police Chief Cassidy Chambers longs for a break from the recent crimes plaguing Lantern Beach. She simply wants to enjoy her friends' upcoming wedding, to prepare for the busy tourist season about to slam the island, and to gather all the dirt she can on the suspicious community that's invaded the town. But trouble explodes on the island, sending residents—including Cassidy—into a squall of uneasiness. Cassidy may have more than one enemy plotting her demise, and the collateral damage seems unthinkable. As the temperature rises, so does the pressure to find answers. Someone is determined that Lantern Beach would be better off without their new police chief. And for Cassidy, one wrong move could mean certain death.

Dead on Arrival

With a highly charged local election consuming the community, Police Chief Cassidy Chambers braces herself for a challenging day of breaking up petty conflicts and tamping down high emotions. But when widespread food poisoning spreads among potential voters across the island, Cassidy smells something rotten in the air. As Cassidy examines every possibility to uncover what's going on, local enigma Anthony Gilead again comes on her radar. The man is running for mayor and his cult-like following is growing at an alarming rate. Cassidy feels certain he has a spy embedded in her inner circle. The problem is that her pool of suspects gets deeper every day. Can Cassidy get to the bottom of what's eating away at her peaceful island home? Will voters turn out despite the outbreak of illness plaguing their tranquil town? And the even bigger question: Has darkness come to stay on Lantern Beach?

Plan of Action

A missing Navy SEAL. Danger at the boiling point. The ultimate showdown. When Police Chief Cassidy Chambers' husband, Ty, disappears, her world is turned upside down. His truck is discovered with blood inside, crashed in a ditch on Lantern Beach, but he's nowhere to be found. As they launch a manhunt to find him, Cassidy discovers that someone on the island has a deadly obsession with Ty. Meanwhile, Gilead's Cove seems to be imploding. As danger heightens, federal law enforcement officials are called in. The cult's growing threat could lead to the pinnacle standoff of good versus evil. A clear plan of action is needed or the results will be devastating. Will Cassidy find Ty in time, or will she face a gut-wrenching loss? Will Anthony Gilead finally be unmasked for who he really is and be brought to justice? Hundreds of innocent lives are at stake . . . and not everyone will come out alive.

LANTERN BEACH ESCAPE

Afterglow

What if you married someone, only to discover that she was suspected of killing her former fiancé? While on their honeymoon, Grayson and Rachel Stewart are confronted with dark details of Rachel's past. As more facts begin emerging, their new marriage is thrown into a tailspin. The newlyweds must figure out how to move forward . . . and Grayson must figure out if he married a killer.

LANTERN BEACH BLACKOUT

Dark Water

Colton Locke can't forget the black op that went terribly wrong. Desperate for a new start, he moves to Lantern Beach, North Carolina, and forms Blackout, a private security firm. Despite his hero status, he can't erase the mistakes he's made. For the past year, Elise Oliver hasn't been able to shake the feeling that there's more to her husband's death than she was told. When she finds a hidden box of his personal possessions, more questions—and suspicions—arise. The only person she trusts to help her is her husband's best friend, Colton Locke. Someone wants Elise dead. Is it because she knows too much? Or is it to keep her from finding the truth? The Blackout team must uncover dark secrets hiding beneath seemingly still waters. But those very secrets might just tear the team apart.

Safe Harbor

Guilt over past mistakes haunts former Navy SEAL Dez Rodriguez. When he's asked to guard a pop star during a music festival on Lantern Beach, he's all set for what he hopes is a breezy assignment. Bree hasn't found fame to be nearly as fulfilling as she dreamed. Instead, she's more like a carefully crafted character living out a pre-scripted story. When a stalker's threats become deadly, her life—and career—are turned upside down. From the start, Bree sees her temporary bodyguard as a player, and Dez sees Bree as a spoiled rich girl. But when they're thrown together in a fight for survival, both must learn to trust. Can Dez protect Bree—and his carefully guarded heart? Or will their safe harbor ultimately become their death trap?

Ripple Effect

Griff McIntyre never expected his ex-wife and three-year-old daughter to come to Lantern Beach. After an abduction attempt, they're desperate for safety. Now Griff's not letting either of them out of his sight. Bethany knows Griff is the only one who can protect them, despite the fact that he broke her heart. But she'll do anything to keep her daughter safe—even if it means playing nicely with a man she can't stand. As peril ripples through their lives, Griff and Bethany must work together to protect their daughter. But an unseen enemy wants something from them . . . and will stop at nothing to get it. When disaster strikes, can Griff keep his family safe? Or will past mistakes bring the ultimate failure?

Rising Tide

Benjamin James knows there's a traitor within his former command. The rest of his team might even think it's him. As danger closes in, he must clear himself and stop a deadly plot by a dangerous terrorist group. All CJ Compton wanted was a new start after her career ended under suspicion. Working as the house manager for private security group Blackout seems perfect. But there's more trouble here than what she left behind. As the tide rushes in, the stakes continue to rise. If the Blackout team fails, it's not just Lantern Beach at stake—it's the whole country. Can Benjamin and CJ overcome their differences and work together to find the truth?

LANTERN BEACH GUARDIANS

Hide and Seek

During a turbulent storm, a child is found on the beach, washed up from the ocean. Making matters worse—the girl can't speak. Lantern Beach Police Chief Cassidy Chambers can feel the danger lurking around them. As more mysterious incidents happen on the island, Cassidy fears each crime is somehow connected to this child—a child no one has reported missing. Cassidy knows the girl's life depends on finding answers. With the help of her husband, Ty, a former Navy SEAL, she scrambles to discover what exactly is going on. Someone appears to be playing a deadly version of hide-and-seek—and using the girl as a pawn. But what will happen when the game finally ends? *Hide and Seek is the first book in a three book series. Though the main storyline of each book will be wrapped up at the end, some plot lines will not be resolved until the end of book three.*

Shock and Awe

They thought the worst was over—but they were wrong.When Police Chief Cassidy Chambers arrives at a grisly crime scene, she's shocked at where the evidence leads. Then the threats start coming. Threats against her. Threats that could upend her life.As more clues are uncovered, a sinister plot is revealed, and Cassidy fears the little girl in her care may be tangled in a deadly scheme. Cassidy and her husband, Ty, will do anything to protect the child, each other, and the island. But what happens when they might not be able to save all three?

Safe and Sound

A call for help draws Police Chief Cassidy Chambers deep into a wooded, isolated area on Lantern Beach. What she finds shakes her to the core—a friend is bleeding out, and his last words before dying are: They know. Figuring out who killed her friend and what his final words meant becomes Cassidy's mission. Have members of the notorious gang that placed a bounty on her head discovered her new life? Or is someone else trying to teach her a twisted lesson? Elements from past investigations surface and threaten more than one person's safety. Cassidy and her husband, Ty, must make sense of the deadly secrets that unfold at every turn. If not, the life they've built together might come to a permanent end.

LANTERN BEACH BLACKOUT: THE NEW RECRUITS

Rocco

Former Navy SEAL and new Blackout recruit Rocco Foster is on a simple in and out mission. But

the operation turns complicated when an unsuspecting woman wanders into the line of fire. Peyton
Ellison's life mission is to sprinkle happiness on
those around her. When a cupcake delivery turns into
a fight for survival, she must trust her rescuer—a
handsome stranger—to keep her safe. Rocco is determined to figure out why someone is targeting
Peyton. First, he must keep the intriguing woman
safe and earn her trust. But threats continue to
pummel them as incriminating evidence emerges
and pits them against each other. With time running
out, the two must set aside both their growing attraction and their doubts about each other in order to
work together. But the perilous facts they discover
leave them wondering what exactly the truth is . . .
and if the truth can be trusted.

Axel

*Women are missing. Private security firm Blackout
must find them before another victim disappears.* Axel
Hendrix likes to live on the edge. That's why being a
Navy SEAL suited him so well. But after his last
mission, he cut his losses and joined Blackout
instead. His team's latest case involves an undercover investigation on Lantern Beach. Olivia Rollins
came to the island to escape her problems—and
danger. When trouble from her past shows up in

town, she impulsively blurts she's engaged to Axel, the womanizing man she's seen while waitressing. Now, she may not be the only one in danger. So could Axel. Axel knows Olivia might be his chance to find answers and that acting like her fiancé is the perfect cover for his latest assignment. But he doesn't like throwing Olivia into the middle of such a dangerous situation. Nor is he comfortable with the feelings she stirs inside him. With Olivia's life—as well as both their hearts—on the line, Axel must uncover the truth and stop an evil plan before more lives are destroyed.

Beckett

When the daughter of a federal judge is abducted, private security firm Blackout must find her. Psychologist Samantha Reynolds doesn't know why someone is targeting her. Even after a risky mission to save her, danger still lingers. She's determined to use her insights into the human mind to help decode the deadly clues being left in the wake of her rescue. Former Navy SEAL Beckett Jones needs to figure out who's responsible for the crimes hounding Sami. He's not sure why he's so protective of the woman he rescued, but he'll do anything to keep her safe—even if it means risking his heart. As the body count rises, there's no room for error. Beckett and Sami must both tear down the careful walls they've built around themselves in order to survive. If they don't figure out who's responsible, the madman will continue his death spree . . . and one of them might be next.

Gabe

When former Navy SEAL and current Blackout operative Gabe Michaels is almost killed in a hit-and-run, the aftermath completely upends his life. He's no longer safe—and he's not the only one. Dr. Autumn Spenser came to Lantern Beach to start fresh. But while treating Gabe after his accident, she senses there's more to what happened to him than meets the eye. When she digs deeper into his past, she never expects to be drawn into a deadly dilemma. Gabe has been infatuated with the pretty doctor since the day they met. Now, can he keep her from harm? Could someone out of his league ever return his feelings or will her past hurts keep them apart? As danger continues to pummel them, Gabe and Autumn are thrown together in a quest to find answers. More important than their growing attraction, they must stay alive long enough to stop the person desperate to destroy them.

LANTERN BEACH MAYDAY

Run Aground

A dead captain on a luxury yacht leads to a tumultuous seafaring journey . . . Med student Kenzie Anderson, tired of letting others chart her future, accepts a job as second steward aboard Almost Paradise. But when she finds the captain dead before the charter even begins, her plans seem to capsize. Jimmy James Gamble senses something vulnerable and slightly naive about Kenzie when he finds her on the docks. Realizing danger may still be lingering close, he uses his hidden skills to earn a place on the charter. But being there causes him to risk everything—especially as more suspicious incidents occur. As they set out to sea, Kenzie and Jimmy James both wonder if they're in over their heads. They must figure out how to stop a killer before anyone onboard is hurt . . . otherwise, both their futures might just run aground.

Dead Reckoning

A yachtie fears for her life when she's the only witness to a murder . . . Kenzie Anderson knows what she saw at the harbor—a woman strangled and pushed overboard. But there's no proof of a crime . . . only her word. Jimmy James Gamble believes Kenzie, even if no one else does. As he senses the danger in the air, all he wants is to keep her away from any more trouble—especially after their last charter. Either Kenzie or the yacht they're working on seem to be a magnet for murder and mayhem. Someone is willing to kill to get what he wants—and will do so again if necessary. Can Jimmy James and Kenzie navigate these unfamiliar waters? Or will relying on dead reckoning lead them to their deaths?

Tipping Point

Awakening in a boat surrounded by nothing but water, a yachtie has no doubt someone wants her dead. Kenzie Anderson is determined not to let anyone scare her away from completing the charter season—even with the threats on her life. The only person she can trust is Captain Jimmy James Gamble, despite their tumultuous relationship. Kenzie and Jimmy James both suspect turbulent currents rush beneath the tranquil surface aboard the luxury yacht Almost Paradise. Secrets seem to abound, each one increasing the tension aboard the boat. As answers rise to the surface, neither Kenzie nor Jimmy James is prepared for what they find. Have they both reached their tipping points? Their adversaries want nothing more than to make Kenzie disappear . . . forever. It may be too late for a mayday call.

LANTERN BEACH CHRISTMAS

Silent Night

Catch up with your favorite Lantern Beach characters as they come together to help the town's beloved police chief. On the night before Christmas Eve, as she begins her maternity leave, Lantern Beach Police Chief Cassidy Chambers disappears. Suspecting foul play, law enforcement officers combine forces with the Blackout Security team and island residents to find her. Despite a snowstorm in his path, Cassidy's husband, Ty, desperately tries to return home in time to save her. With his wife's and baby's lives on the line, he needs a Christmas miracle. Will the tightknit community of Lantern Beach be able to rescue their beloved police chief in time? Or will Cassidy's cries for help be met only with silence?

LANTERN BEACH BLACKOUT: DANGER RISING

Brandon

Physically he's protecting her. But emotionally she's never felt more exposed. The last person tech heiress Finley Cooper ever wanted to see again was Brandon Hale. Two years ago, Brandon shattered her heart. Now Finley needs protection, and, against her wishes, Brandon is assigned the job. Even worse, they must pretend to be a couple in order to find answers. Brandon, a former Navy SEAL, met Finley while on an undercover assignment in Ecuador. But he broke her trust, and now he doesn't blame Finley for hating him. As a new Blackout operative, Brandon's first assignment throws him into Finley's life 24/7. Someone wants her dead, and it's clear this person won't stop until that mission is accomplished. To keep her safe, Brandon must regain Finley's trust. Can he convince her she's more than a job to him? Or will peril permanently silence them?

Dylan

His job is to protect her. The trouble is . . . she doesn't want protection. Former Navy SEAL Dylan Granger's new assignment requires him to use both his tactical abilities and his acting skills. Hired by Katie Logan's father, his job is to protect the gutsy university professor while concealing his identity. To maintain his cover, he takes the unassuming role of her new assistant. Katie—a disgraced reporter—has stumbled upon a lead she can't ignore. Now it's clear someone is targeting her, but she refuses to back down. Her handsome new assistant is a welcome distraction from the chaos. But Dylan's skillset goes way beyond his job description, and Katie begins to suspect there's more to Dylan than he's letting on. Dylan's mission can't be disclosed—not if he wants to keep

Katie safe. But as his feelings for her grow and the danger increases, keeping his secret becomes more of a challenge than he ever imagined. With innocent lives on the line, Dylan must choose between protecting Katie or savings others.

Maddox

He's on the case . . . and she's his prime suspect. Classified technology is missing, a delivery driver is dead, and former Navy SEAL Maddox King must find the culprits before a dangerous plan is enacted. To find answers, the Blackout agent must go undercover as a maintenance man at millionaire Seymore Whitlock's estate. While there, he sets his sights on Whitlock's personal assistant, Taryn Parsons, a woman who has everything to gain and nothing to lose. Six months ago, Whitlock plucked Taryn out of obscurity to become his caretaker. But with deadly incidents haunting the estate, Taryn doesn't know who she can trust—including the new maintenance man who is both intriguing . . . and unnerving. The stakes continue to escalate, and Maddox is running out of time to find answers. With the body count rising along with his list of suspects, this assignment may be his most challenging yet . . . for both his skillset and his heart.

Titus

She shattered his heart once. Can he set her betrayal aside for the sake of his country? The last person Titus Armstrong wants to join forces with is the woman who dumped him for his brother, Alex. But Presley Lennox is Blackout's best chance at infiltrating a dangerous organization known as The System and finding out more about their deadly plans. Presley Lennox wants out—of both an abusive relationship and the radical group she's become entangled with because of Alex. When Titus reappears in her life, he's like an answer to prayer—until he asks her to dive deeper into the very life she's been trying to escape. A dangerous plan is brewing that could destroy thousands of lives. Titus and Presley may be the only ones who can stop what's about to be unleashed. Failure would mean certain chaos . . . not only for them but for their nation.

BEACH BOUND BOOKS AND BEANS MYSTERIES

Bound by Murder

When widow Talitha Robinson buys an old store on the boardwalk in Lantern Beach, North Carolina, she's in for a surprise . . . or several. She plans to renovate the space and open Beach Bound Books and

Beans, but never expects to find a decades-old skeleton hidden inside one of the walls. As word of the discovery spreads across the island, strange occurrences begin to occur around her. It soon becomes clear someone still knows something about the dead person—something they don't want discovered. Thankfully, former police chief and current mayor Mac MacArthur seems just as eager to unravel the mystery behind the skeletal remains as Tali. But as the two bind together to solve the case, a devastating secret is revealed. Will their newfound friendship come unglued before they find the answers to the past? Or will their blooming relationship die like the man hidden in the wall?Bound by Murder is book 1 in a four book series of novellas. Though the main mystery is resolved, there are threads that will continue throughout the entire series.

Bound by Disaster

Talitha Robinson is knee-deep in renovations as she prepares to open her new bookstore when a body washes ashore on Lantern Beach. While news of the suspicious death surges across the island, a stranger comes knocking on Tali's door, begging her to endorse his unfinished suspense novel. Unable to dissuade the author, Tali is left holding his manuscript in her hands. But she has no idea of the peril written on its pages. Mac MacArthur has kept his distance from Tali since they uncovered a shocking connection about their pasts. But when someone begins to act out the murderous scenes from the book, one victim at a time, Mac's protective instincts override his decision to stay away. As danger escalates, Mac and Tali must manage their conflicting feelings as they work together to stop this killer . . . before the last chapter is written.

Bound by Mystery

Talitha Robinson is well on her way to completing renovations for her new bookstore, Beach Bound Books and Beans, in Lantern Beach, North Carolina. But when she hosts a friendly meet-and-greet with bookstore owners from nearby islands, the progress she's making comes to a deadly end. Someone is backstabbed—literally—right under Tali's nose. To make matters worse, Tali's finger-prints are all over the murder weapon and a neighbor claims to have seen Tali commit the crime. Mac MacArthur knows Tali isn't the type to hurt anyone, but it doesn't take a former police chief to figure out things don't look good for her. The two work together to read between the lines and decipher the truth before Tali gets locked away for crimes she didn't commit. As more evidence stacks up, it becomes clear that someone wants to take Tali out of the story. For good.

Bound by Trouble

With the grand opening of Beach Bound Books and Beans, Tali Robinson's dreams are finally coming true. She hopes to now put the past behind her and start a new chapter. When a suspicious stranger mysteriously shows up at her celebration, her hopes disappear faster than a bestseller at a book signing.Mac MacArthur is ready to solidify his relationship with Tali. But mending their differences is easier said than done. Then someone sets their sights on Tali—and wants to put her out of print . . . permanently. With trouble brewing, Tali and Mac have no choice but to dive into the chaos of the past. However, as more answers are revealed, the danger increases. The truth will come at a great cost . . . one that will bind them together or drive them apart.

Bound by Mayhem

As cast and crew members prepare for Lantern Beach's first annual Christmas play, catastrophe strikes. Abby Mendez, the director and brainchild behind the play, never shows up for a dress rehearsal. Threats emerge, and it becomes clear that not everyone on the island feels the Christmas spirit.

With dangerous encounters and ghostly disappearing acts threatening not only the play but also the safety of Lantern Beach residents, former police chief Mac MacArthur and Abby's friend Tali Robinson jump in to help. The stakes rise as the perpetrator continues to haunt Abby's past, torment her present, and threaten her future. When it seems all hope is nearly lost, can the people of Lantern Beach work together to save the play? Or will this phantom scrooge steal the final act?

USA Today has called Christy Barritt's books "scary, funny, passionate, and quirky."

Christy writes both mystery and romantic suspense novels that are clean with underlying messages of faith. Her books have sold more than four million copies and have won the Daphne du Maurier Award for Excellence in Suspense and Mystery, have been twice nominated for the Romantic Times Reviewers' Choice Award, and have finaled for both a Carol Award and Foreword Magazine's Book of the Year.

She is married to her Prince Charming, a man who thinks she's hilarious—but only when she's not trying to be. Christy is a self-proclaimed klutz, an avid music lover who's known for spontaneously bursting into song, and a road trip aficionado.

When she's not working or spending time with her family, she enjoys singing, playing the guitar, and exploring small, unsuspecting towns where people have no idea how accident-prone she is.

Find Christy online at:
    www.christybarritt.com
    www.facebook.com/christybarritt
    www.twitter.com/cbarritt

Sign up for Christy's newsletter to get information on all of her latest releases here: **www.christybarritt. com/newsletter-sign-up/**

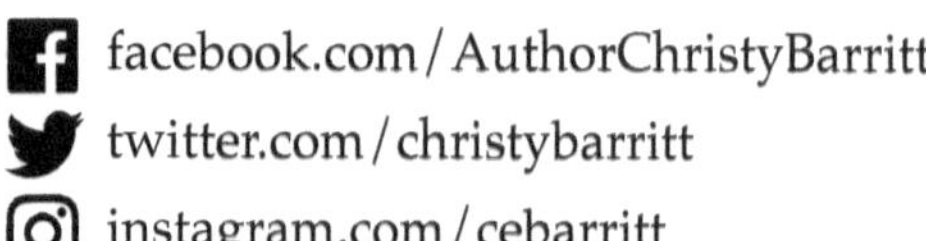

facebook.com / AuthorChristyBarritt
twitter.com / christybarritt
instagram.com / cebarritt